The Ghost of Lantern Bridge

A Perry Normal Adventure Book 5

Mason Stone

Dedicated to all those who love bedtime stories, especially the creepy kind.

To Pig, my one and only.

<u>Disclaimer</u>

This is a work of fiction, and the depiction of persons, places and circumstances is fictional. This material, however, is based on both anecdotal and factual records and accounts. Any relationship to real persons or organizations is purely coincidental.

Contents

PART I   THE LEGEND BEGINS

CHAPTER ONE   LANTERN BRIDGE

"What is it?"

"Darned if I know," said Perry, "but it's coming closer. Do you think it knows we are here, Henry?"

"I sure hope not. I mean if that's what I think it is, I don't want anything to do with it!"

Henry's flashlight was not working. He smacked it a couple of times as if that would refresh the batteries or jog the bulb into life. No dice.

"The lantern, Henry! See it? Whoever it is--is swinging a lantern, lit by candles looks like. Is it looking for something?"

The shadowy figure was moving the light to and fro from the rail of the bridge, as if trying to cast light on the dark pools beneath.

"Yeah, maybe Perry—but what? Is this related to the story of the Ghost of Lantern Bridge? I m-mean, that *is* a ghost we're looking at, isn't it Perry?"

***

It was late in the year, near Halloween, and the red and gold leaves from the forest trees were falling and covering the ground in striking color only seen at this time of year. Pumpkins were ripe and found their way onto every porch and into every window as the festival drew near.

Perry Normal and his school companions were still eager to participate even though they were getting a bit old to trick-or-treat.

Classrooms and halls at Brackendale Middle School were festooned with ribbons of orange and black, costumes were designed in classrooms and study areas for the big upcoming annual party that turned the cafeteria into a swirling sea of goblins and ghosts, vampires and superheroes. It was generally agreed that this was one of the highlights of the school year.

There are many bridges in New York State, and upstate New York has its share--some are steel and concrete, some are ancient covered wood bridges in the Colonial style. Most span a creek or stream that traverses the local farm country, flowing north to Lake Ontario, or east to Lake Cayuga.

Some have unusual legends or lore about them: some are said to be haunted, and locals take this seriously since everybody knows the old saying: "Where there's smoke, there's fire!"

Lantern Bridge was just such a bridge. Its name came from the occasional and mysterious appearance of a lantern lit in the blackness of night on a country road. By whom it was carried was the subject of conjecture by both children and adults of Cayuga County. Some say it was a ghostly warning to drive carefully on these two-lane roads; some say it was merely fireflies or some similar natural phenomenon and had no significance at all. There were as many opinions as people in local taverns and churches.

Few travelers went this way; most took Highway 20 or drive to the I-90 if they were going to Rochester to the west, or Syracuse to the east. On County Road 13 a few isolated farmsteads and an old church could be found east of town, all that remained of a New York that was first Dutch—then British, and finally—American.

History tells that two days march east of here, the British and their Iroquois allies fought desperately with the Continental Army of George Washington which was fighting for its very existence against the mightiest army in the world. Some say on such nights

the wind would blow and ghostly figures of
Revolutionary soldiers would appear by moonlight—
tramping home on foot or horseback, home to these
farms and stables and villages in the region of the
Finger Lakes.

On such nights, townfolk stayed indoors, close to the
fireplace, close to the kitchen where light and warmth
shut out the shivery darkness.

One such family was the family of Perry Normal who
lived with his parents and older sister in a tidy
middle-class neighborhood just inside the town limits.

Perry was a keen 8th Grade student at Brackendale
Middle School and was the school's Science champion.
He had been honored as winner of the Stateside
Science Fair and had been an Astronomy intern at JPL
in Pasadena the previous summer. He was liked by
everybody—teachers, friends, and peers.

He had even found ancient artifacts while on a
summer diving holiday in Florida that were now in
the local museum of American History. Everyone in
town and even beyond knew about this remarkable
boy.

Some of them, very few really, knew that he was also
prone to having—how shall we say it? Extraordinary

experiences. Quite extraordinary. Time travel… strange things seen in Space through a telescope… lost civilizations… Near-Death Experiences. Oh yes! Perry Normal was someone to keep an eye on! You never knew what might happen when he was around.

***

Perry and his 'gang' (as people called them) liked to hang around The Malt Shop, a local cafe that had been serving good old American diner food for years— nearly sixty years to be exact. Late-night people like truckers or taxi drivers came there after dark. Families came for Sunday brunch. And students came most days after school just to eat and gab, and find comfort in each other's company.

"What are you going as?" Rita asked Charmaine.

"I'm going as a princess," Charmaine said.

"Trick or treating?" said Max. "I'm too old."

"No, silly!" Charmaine replied. "To the party at Katya's house. No boys invited, by the way."

"That's discrimination," said Robert, gobbling his usual plate of fries and gravy.

"I'm wondering what we should do for the school party," said Margot.

"I almost forgot," said Max.

"I'm going to ask Miss Floon if I can carve a jack o' lantern and put it in the library window," Rita said.

"Let's ask her if we can decorate the whole library for Halloween," said Charmaine.

"Maybe she should dress up as a witch for the day," said Robert.

"That's so mean!" Rita and Charmaine scowled at Robert, who shrugged and went back to his plate of fries.

"Hey! Where is Perry? Where is Henry? Anybody know?" Max half-rose in his seat as if the two science geeks of the school were huddled in some corner discussing The Neumann Resonance or something.

"Don't know," said the girls.

"Good question!" said Robert.

"They're up to something," Charmaine opined, "I can just feel it."

***

The next day at school there was a test, and the halls were unusually quiet. It seemed like all the teachers

get together in the staff room and plan how to wreck
an entire week of school with all kinds of tests.

"Why do they do this? Don't they know we are half
worked to death already? Why does every single class
have to have a test in the same week?" Charmaine
was always vocal about her feelings, and this was no
exception. Many students felt she spoke for all of
them too shy or immature to speak up.

Charmaine had grown up a lot this year. Her summer
experience in emergency response training at a local
military base had brought new challenges to her, and
to all the gang. It was on a rescue mission during a
weekend of brutal storms in the area that she came
face-to-face with a dead person. Two of them,
actually: one was the unfortunate bus driver who was
killed by falling steel from a power line; the other was
a boy of about six and half who smacked his head
when the bus crashed and did not recover.

Things like that change somebody. Charmaine had a
deeper personal side that few seldom saw, but those
who knew her saw in her eyes a reflective girl, an
older girl. Perhaps that is why the gang trusted her
even more than before.

"Perry! We were looking for you yesterday at The Malt Shop!" Charmaine had Perry by the collar and playfully tugged him off balance.

"I'll tell you tomorrow," Perry said. "Henry and I had a mission to fulfill. We gotta run to the Socials test. C'mon, Charmaine."

"Now class, this test is going to be multiple choice so I want you to fill in the bubble card properly—in pencil."

Mr. Rhys-Jones—who was from Wales-- was a stickler for procedure. He was kind of new at Brackendale and the kids did not know him that well, so they just did what he said—which is what teachers usually want anyway.

"What the hell?!" Mike and the Gorilla—both of whom always sat at the back from which point of view they could harass or prank anyone, both muttered at once. "There's sixty questions here. We didn't even learn sixty things so far this semester."

"Quieten down Mike and Randy! No talk of any kind during a test. If there's something you don't understand, raise your hand."

Randy—whose social manners, or lack of them earned him the nickname 'Gorilla'—started to raise his hand but Mike caught it on the way up and pushed it back down.

"I don't understand…I don't understand a damn thing on this test," Randy complained in a whisper.

"Make sure your full name and homeroom are on the front page, and on the scan card, or you are going to give me more work that I don't need," Mr. Rhys-Jones said in that whiny teacher voice.

They probably learn that in Teacher's College many were thinking. This test was hard! They all were thinking *that*.

In order to permit students to survive the test week, the principal directed the exam timetable to be restricted to two tests per day maximum. Free time was devoted to study, or outdoor activity like football or soccer in the back field.

For non-athletes, it meant either time in the library, the cafeteria, or the smokehole for those who were desperate for a cigarette.

But in every corner of Brackendale Middle School there was a friendly face, a high-five, a smile that reminded you that this was a community, a place where you belonged and were safe. You had to go to Brackendale to fully appreciate that.

Chapter Two   The Hitchhiker

It was Friday. The last exam had been written and submitted; the week of torture was over!

The gang was stuffed into every bench and booth at The Malt Shop which after all kind of belonged to them anyway. The owner Dave knew that. Other customers sat out front on the stools or at the tables near the kitchen; the Brackendale gang sat in back, a warm cozy space for winter days, all kinds of days.

Dave himself often greeted them; his wife cooked and was seldom seen unless she ducked out behind the kitchen for a smoke. But she was really nice, too.

   " Hey! Listen everyone! I've got a story to tell you that will totally freak you out. Dave himself told me, and a local highway patrolman told him."

Max was playing to the audience.

   "Okay, okay...spit it out!" Mike and Randy had their own kind of gang to hang out with, but from time to time lurked in the back with everyone else, enjoying the unbelievably tasty diner fare Dave's wife Wanda served up.

"Do you believe in ghosts?" Max started off.

At that precise moment, Perry and Henry drifted in.

"I do—I mean *we* do," said Henry looking at their faces.

"Totally!" said Perry sliding in to the last empty booth and speaking softly to the girl who took his order.

"Listen to this!" exulted Max. "Dave told me that the patrolman—Officer Van Cleef I think it was—told him that he had a really unnerving experience out on County Road 13."

You could have heard a pin drop!

"Out by Lantern Bridge." Max paused, looking a little frightened actually.

"The officer was on patrol in mid-August, a few nights after that crash that killed Sylvia Martin. You know? The one where her dipshit boyfriend drove his car off the bridge into the creek? Killed her, but not himself? He was too drunk to remember any of it, and some people in town said he should've died, instead of that girl."

"I remember that," said Randy. "That guy was some asshole from over in Fernville who dropped out of high school."

"Well let me get to the ghost part," Max continued.

"Officer Van Cleef pulled up to the bridge and parked, and lit a smoke when all of a sudden he saw someone coming toward him on the bridge itself. Only whoever it was--was dressed in white and their feet were at least a yard off the ground."

"What are you saying?" Rita cut in. "She was a ghost?"

"Do you know anybody else who floats as they walk, and that you can see right through in the moonlight?" Max was firmly in control.

"Is that what the policeman said?" asked Katya, who was clinging to Margot—head down--at this point.

"*Right through!*" said Max. "And then he noticed something else. A car came up the bridge from behind him and its lights caught the girl in the beam, and she had her thumb out like she was hitchhiking."

"Where do ghosts *go* at midnight?" Robert said in his usual snarky way.

"I don't wanna know!" said Katya.

"What did the cop do?" said Mike.

"He did a one-eighty and hightailed it outta there," Max said. "What would *you* do?"

"The same thing," said Mike. "For sure."

"And where do you think he would drive to get a coffee and relax his nerves?" Max said.

"The Malt Shop." Everyone spoke at the same time.

"Exactly," said Max.

"So that's how Dave got the story, huh?" Henry was in the conversation now.

"But why did Dave tell *you*?" Randy asked.

"Let's just say that...I have my sources who tell me stuff," Max smiled.

"Perry? What do you think?" Charmaine really wanted to know what the resident scientist in their little group was thinking.

"Well, it is quite a coincidence that this comes up, because Henry and I are following up a story that we heard from Bob Caygeon—the museum curator. He told us a story about a ghost as well. And I'm thinking that these two ghost stories might be intertwined somehow. I don't know, but it's a feeling I'm getting."

"You're going to tell us what possible scientific basis for believing in spirits there is, yes?" said Robert.

"That requires more hot chocolate and maybe a sandwich," teased Perry.

"I'll pay," said Robert. Robert had rich parents who regularly gave him an outrageous allowance which he apparently mostly spent on his friends.

"Well, here's what I think," Perry began.

"Although the science is scanty, the evidence overwhelmingly suggests that ghosts are real and may well be just what people say they are: phantom forms of those who have died, especially died violently."

"Really?" Rita spoke now.

"Henry and I have been doing research on ghostly phenomena since last year, and there are distinct patterns in anecdotal reports…".

Randy cut in. "What's *anecdotal*?"

"Means a personal experience that someone tells you," Perry replied.

"Ghosts are part of folklore in every country—from Iceland to Indonesia. Because Science wants proof of a tangible kind, paranormal researchers are now collecting infrared video, Electronic Voice Phenomena, and events that can be recorded and reviewed over and over. Photographs of orbs and apparitions are getting hard to dismiss as lens flares or equipment glitches."

"Henry, didn't you get film of that ghost we saw, the girl with pearls?" Max had a good memory. Last year they had witnessed a ghostly haunting of a local bridge and Henry had hazy video of the spirit walking in the moonlight.

"I did, although it is not conclusive evidence all by itself," Henry admitted. "But me? I think it was real."

Everyone nodded in agreement.

"So you see?" said Max excitedly. "Ghosts exist and ghosts want to say something, bring us a message from the Beyond."

"Yeah," said Robert, "Don't go for a ride with a guy that is drunk!"

"I think that if this *is* the ghost or spirit of poor Sylvia, we should do something for her," said Charmaine, her face looking quite serious.

"Like what?" said Randy.

"Like try to find out what she wants, why she is…well…hanging around Lantern Bridge. If we assume she is who we think she is, she will know we want to help her. Am I right?"

"Definitely," said Max.

"And if Perry is right—and he usually is—then there is purpose for us helping a lost soul who cannot go to Heaven, or whatever." Charmaine was firm.

"Do we have to do this at Halloween?" said Katya.

"This is the best time to do it," said Robert, and apparently Mike and Randy and Max were in agreement with that since they were smiling and pumping their fists up and down.

"This is getting real, you guys," said Randy. "We are talking about stalking a ghost that haunts an old bridge to make contact from the spirit world so we can take some action in the physical world on their behalf. Are we freakin' serious?"

Charmaine placed her hand palm up on the table,
looked at each one of them and said: "Are you in?"
Seven other hands were laid atop hers.

"Alright," she said.

Henry Gerrit Schuyler lived around the corner from Perry Normal and his family. They had been close friends since First Grade, and had become resident geniuses at Brackendale Middle School with exceedingly high grades, particularly in Science and Math, and well-known participants in Science festivities including the New York State Science Fair where they placed first among many statewide candidates.

Henry's father's family were Old Dutch who had settled in New York in the days of New Amsterdam and Peter Stuyvesant, long before the British took control of the colony. His mother was similarly a descendent of Dutch settlers along the Hudson who gave their names to villages and communities like Peekskill and the Catskills. Their roots in America were old and deep.

"Dad, do we have any ancestors who might have fought in the Revolutionary War?" Henry was cross-legged on the living room floor after a fine Sunday dinner in October.

"That's an interesting question, Henry," Peter Schuyler responded. "I've often wondered, and I got to ask your great-grandfather before his passing the very same question."

Curiously, Henry's father pulled his legs up on the couch in a cross-legged manner as well, which psychologists call 'mirroring'—a kind of body language that confirms the rapport between two speakers.

"He told me that there was a family legend that a Schuyler was somehow involved in the heroic defense of Fort Stanwix—over Rome way nowadays."

"Go on."

"Well, the British were trying to cut off New England and force a surrender, but George Washington and the Continental Army had other ideas. I don't know as much as I should but the British were defeated again and again by American colonial militia.

From what I understand, Fort Stanwix was one of those situations. I was told that Major General Philip Schuyler was in charge of defending the fort against British troops from Quebec, who were aided by local Iroquois from the Seneca and Mohawk nations."

"So we are related to this general guy—who beat back the British?" Henry was leaning forward and rocking on his folded legs.

"Well, I can only tell you what I was told, Henry. Sounds like a bedtime story rather than historical fact to me. But you know--you and your friend Perry could do some digging around and maybe there's something to it."

"Let's have him over for dinner sometime soon, Henry," his mother said. "We haven't seen him in ages."

"Cool! I'm going upstairs to study for the term tests next week. I will text Perry and mention all this. I have a feeling he's going to have an idea about where we can start. I can't believe I may be related to a Revolutionary war hero," Henry was muttering as he went upstairs to his room.

Unlike Perry—who had an older sister—Henry was an only child, and had adapted to living in his own little world of books, and collections of rocks and gems, chemistry equipment, and assorted oddities like microscopes and slides of cells. There would not have been room for a sibling up there—two of the three bedrooms were science labs in the making.

"You know Henry, this might be a perfect excuse: we have to do a History project this year, and of course the department prefers we do American history. We can investigate this whole thing about the Fort Stanwix thing since it is tied into the history of New York State before it was a state.

And we can start with a visit to the Museum of American History right here in Brackendale. The curator Mr. Caygeon loves us since we brought him that stuff from Florida, that ancient tablet with the mysterious script. He knows lots of stuff about the old days in New York. What do you think, Henry?"

"Awesome. Let's pick a day to drop by there, maybe after the Math exam, and see what he can tell us."

"Speaking of which, I tried to explain Venn diagrams to Rita, Max and Katya...but they still don't get it. It's so simple--my Mom could get it. Anyhow, call me if you get stuck on something. Don't forget there will be a ten-mark question on using Base Two instead of Base Ten."

"'kay, Perry. Later."

***

"Well, what I *can* tell you is that a number of volunteers for the Continental Army came from Upper New York, and some from right around here."

The curator Bob Caygeon was taking Perry and Henry on a little walking tour of the museum area devoted to New York State and its part in American history.

"Here for example is a soldier dressed in the uniform of the time, holding his musket, and surrounded by his basic kit: powder flask, musket balls, canteen, bedroll, change of socks and so on."

"Wow," Henry exclaimed. "The three-cornered hat—tricorne is it? I always wanted one of those!"

"Yeah that would make a great Halloween outfit," Perry said. "Why do they wear white breeches and waistcoats? Even their shirts were somewhat white."

"They regarded themselves as honorable representatives of an emerging nation; they wanted to look as decent as the Redcoats or the Hessians, who had a long military tradition. Look at their shoes: black shoes with buckles. Like they were on parade instead of slogging through swampy forests full of bugs and snakes."

Mr. Caygeon took them to the next display.

"Here is a journal kept by one soldier who lived to return home near Albany. It is leather with stiff yellow paper pages that worked well to absorb the homemade ink that was scratched onto it with a goose quill. Although the pages are stained, you can still make out the writing—quite fancy with curlicues and swooping letters; of course, the writer must have been schooled in order to be able to write in the first place, and second—to be able to express himself and give an accurate account of what was going on around him.

This is a priceless document, really," said Bob. "That's why we keep it under glass and away from the fingers of visitors."

Henry had a burning question for him.

"Do you know anything about Major General Philip Schuyler who commanded Colonial forces in 1777?"

"A little. Why?"

"Two reasons: one is Perry and I are doing a project on the War and were thinking we should get into some of the big events and battles in our own state."

"And two?" Bob looked curious.

"Well, secondly, I have reason to believe that I am personally related to General Schuyler. And I want to find out if that is true."

"*Really?!* Wouldn't that be *something*!" the curator exclaimed.

"I worked last summer as a volunteer in emergency response training under the National Guard," explained Henry.

"I just had a feeling for the job that I can't explain. I'm thinking that there might be something in my blood, in my background, that attracts me to the military—I felt like a different person when we did drills, when I learned how to use firearms. I can't explain it. I *have to* find out about my possible link to the army of George Washington!"

Henry had somehow grown taller while he spoke, and his voice rang with authority.

"Then I shall do everything in my power to help you, Henry Schuyler," said Mr. Caygeon, who unconsciously swung his right hand to his brow in a salute. He didn't even know he did it until after, and he almost blushed, but it fit the moment.

"Can we come back again once we've made some progress with our project?" Perry asked.

"You are always welcome in my museum, Perry and Henry. Here's my email if you need some specific thing that I might know or be able to direct you toward. Good luck, boys!"

"You never told me that!" Perry said as soon as they were outside.

"Told you what? You know I liked shooting the carbines and pistols at the camp."

"No, Henry—not that. I mean about being related to a Revolutionary War general."

"I had no idea until my Dad just happened to mention it on the weekend. We got talking and he said he heard a story from his great-grandfather about a family tradition that they fought the British in the War of Independence."

"That was 240 years ago, Henry. If, by some extraordinary chance, you *are* related to the General, or someone else name Schuyler in the Continental Army, that person would be your great-great-great grandfather; that's six generations!"

"So what you are saying is that this story is probably bogus?" Henry sounded like his feelings were hurt.

"No, not at all. In fact, I am fascinated more than ever to find out if there is any truth to your family legend, aren't you?"

"Absolutely!" Henry replied. "Just that I have no idea how to trace it back, to find something out that happened to my family nearly three centuries ago."

"Well, we are superb investigators, Henry—are we not?"

"True."

"And if anybody can find out then we are the ones, aren't we Henry? We are the best!"

Henry chuckled. Then he started to imitate Freddy Mercury and Queen, singing: "*We are the champions, we are the champions, no time for lo-sers, 'cause we are the cham-pions, of the worrrrld!!*"

And with that, the two chums hopped on their bicycles and pedaled for home.

The year was 1777. The Continental Army under George Washington had growing pains as recruits from the Thirteen Colonies had to be trained, fed, and organized into local and state regiments of around 750 men each. The pay was minimal, the food was bad, the working conditions were worse—and you had an even chance of either surviving your one-year enlistment, or being buried where you were killed.

The British master plan was to isolate New England by driving a wedge down the Hudson River from south of the Canadian border at Quebec, to New York City and the garrison under General Howe at Manhattan.

The wedge was General Johnny Burgoyne, a dashing British soldier with a huge contingent of Loyalists and soldiers stationed in Montreal. His role was to push south along Lake Champlain to French-built Fort Ticonderoga and occupy the Hudson River headwaters which touched on New Hampshire, Vermont, and upper New York State.

To trap the Continental Army forces of Gen. Philip Schuyler , Burgoyne engaged Brigadier-General Barry St. Leger to move west to Lake Ontario, then south to the mouth of the Mohawk river near Oswego, then proceed east to take Fort Stanwix—driving the Continental Army out and closing the jaws of a vise that would shut George Washington's army right out of northern New England and New York.

"What news, sir?"

"Indian scouts have reported that British redcoats are coming across the lake from Canada. They surely mean to attack our position, and we are little prepared for it." Colonel Peter Gansevoort looked worried.

He shouted to the sentry atop the stockade wall.

 "Guard! Tell the men to send scouts west to Lake Oneida to find out when the British arrive and what their strength is."

"Sir? We have but a hundred men here."

"Major-General Schuyler promised to send reinforcements, Sergeant. He is a man of his word. How is our supply of gunpowder?"

"Hardly enough to last two days. And our water and food are low."

"The British bring cannon—six inch guns, maybe mortars," Colonel Gansevoort said. "We have one. I need a plan, Lieutenant."

"I heard that the units at Fort Dayton had made the progress of the enemy more difficult using an *abatis*—a blockade of crisscrossing timber felled across the road, making movement of wagons and artillery impossible until it was cleared."

Col. Gansevoort pulled on his clay pipe, releasing a long stream of blue fragrant tobacco smoke into the evening air.

"Well? What are you waiting for, Sergeant? Get busy! The British will be on our doorstep and we are by no means ready. Their artillery will blow our wooden palisade to matchsticks!"

***

Ten miles east of Fort Stanwix, Nicholas Herkimer and 800 local militia were trudging through the thick spruce forest from Fort Dayton to a place called Oriskany Creek. Their intention was to bolster the tiny contingent at Ft. Stanwix since word had come that the British were coming down the Mohawk from Lake Ontario and men and muskets were needed to oppose them.

A musket was a smoothbore rifle nearly five feet in length and weighing ten-and-a-half pounds, which was loaded from the muzzle with a .75 caliber ball that could hit a man up to 70 yards away. It could be fired every fifteen seconds and was called a Brown Bess in the British and Loyalist ranks. And it was deadly.

To a soldier—even a militiaman—this was his best friend in battle and most men slept with it by their sides. A triangular bayonet could be fixed at the muzzle end, making it a formidable weapon indeed.

The heat and humidity of August were punishing for men carrying guns, ammunition, other supplies, the mosquitoes and biting flies were a torment as they slogged forward in the early afternoon of August 6, 1777.

Without warning, the storm broke.

"Fire!" A voice thundered from the thicket, and a dozen shots tore through the ranks of Herkimer's militiamen. Some fell backward—dead, and some fell on their faces as if the brush could hide them from gunfire.

"Ambush! Fire at will," shouted Herkimer; then he shrieked as a ball of hot lead ripped through his thigh-- flinging him into the bushes.

Confusion and noise and smoke filled the glade where British redcoats and Iroquois Indians had been hiding only moments before, and now slammed into the ranks of the patriots in a ferocious attack.

The waters of Oriskany Creek turned red. Wounded men fell into the water--some drowned, some lay still.

The Iroquois wielded tomahawks—small battle axes which had wide blades that caused savage wounds. Unlike guns, they required no reload, no time wasted while the enemy fell upon you. These native people were fighting for their traditional homelands and were prepared to defend it with all their might.

By the time the shadows of sunset grew long, many bodies from both sides of the conflict lay flung upon the bloody ground, and the horrific energy of battle had now subsided as men withdrew, going back the way they had come to this awful place, this awful moment in a war that nobody had asked for. It was a war that would eventually give birth to a nation, and in that, something good would come from it after all.

***

The Iroquois people were actually a confederacy of tribes (or nations, as they prefer to be called). Some were Mohawk—as was Joseph Brant and his sister Molly, who joined the colonists who were loyal to the King, and whose army now struggled to retain control of a continent. From Virginia to Quebec, The British were well established in the New World.

The native Americans realized these white men were not leaving, were determined to seize and settle all the lands belonging to not only Iroquois, but many other tribal peoples—Ottawa, Shawnee, Huron, Delaware, Cherokee. To avoid this catastrophe, the Mohawks enlisted as British supporters, and gathered a formidable force in upper New York right to the borders of British Canada.

Mohawk warriors were widely feared by both settlers and other tribes—none could match their ability to fight. It was said a Mohawk man could run all day with a man on his back. They knew the backwoods better that any colonials. This is what made them invaluable to the British.

So it was that Barry St. Leger, British officer in charge of conquering western New York, worked in concert with Gen. Johnny Burgoyne to seal off New England from the rest of the colonies, and defeat George Washington's ragtag Continental Army and restore the colonies to British rule. Joseph and Molly Brant were essential to bringing Iroquois allies along.

It was August 8. Herkimer withdrew south and east, mortally wounded yet victorious in a small way: he had taught the Butler Rangers a sharp lesson. When Capt. Johnson returned to St. Leger's main force outside Ft. Stanwix, he was a few men short.

Worse for the Iroquois, while Johnson was fighting at Oriskany—and before St. Leger's troops had arrived at the fort--Continental commandos raided and plundered the Indian camp, taking blankets, personal items, weapons—anything that would demoralize the natives. They even got their hands on Capt. Johnson's notes and plans for the campaign that his Butler's Rangers were to wage alongside the British.

    "Redcoats cannot protect Indian? Brant's anger showed in his face and voice. "Why we should follow Redcoat leader, then?"

St. Leger could not spare his Indian scouts and fighters, yet he had no answer for Joseph Brant.

After days of clearing brush and logs, his cannon and other artillery were dug into place outside the fort. He asked the native Indians to light fires, and whoop war-cries in order to intimidate the patriots inside.

But without blankets and their basic provisions, the Indians were in no mood to holler and shout. The stars came out over an eerily quiet camp full of tents and small bonfires, waiting for dawn.

***

"Willett! Without reinforcements, without supplies--we cannot endure." Col. Gansevoort stood in the shadows of his quarters, the bowl of his pipe glowing with embers as he smoked.

"Sir?" Lieutenant Colonel Marinus Willett was well aware of the dire straits in which the soldiers of Ft. Stanwix found themselves.

"We must get word to Major-General Schuyler. You must take your Oneida scouts down the Mohawk valley as far as Ft. Dayton. There you will find Schuyler, and perhaps the hero of Ticonderoga— Benedict Arnold, one of Washington's most respected officers. They must hear of our plight!"

"Yes, sir. With any luck, they will have learned of the fight at Oriskany, and have a response in mind for our position here. My men and I will leave before dawn. The mists from the swamps will give us an extra hour of cover. I will not return alone, Colonel!"

Chapter Five   A Secret

"Let's assume that the story your father received from his grandfather has a kernel of truth," Perry was saying to Henry.

"Hey, Perry! I could do one of those DNA testkit things, and find out my ancestry that way."

"Yes, except they don't have the specific details we need to know—they just say you have Northern European ancestry, or Asian ancestry. We already know you have European ancestry—look at your skin and facial features; look at your *name.*"

"True. Besides, we don't DNA from anyone we could prove was in the War or is a confirmed relative of someone in the War. It was just too long ago, long before forensic science even existed." Henry looked downcast.

"We have county records of births and deaths, we have journals in the museum. There must be other Schuylers around who know stuff we don't. Don't you have distant cousins or something, Henry?"

"Yes, actually, they live near Utica off I-90 in a place that the state map identifies as the Town of Schuyler. Look!"

Henry was on Google Maps and zoomed in on central New York where the Mohawk River still flows to the Hudson.

"There's Fort Herkimer right there," Henry exclaimed. "I found out it was built in 1740 and it's now a state monument. We could email them and see if they have some leads."

The boys busied themselves with their laptops until dinner time.

"You want to ask your mom if you can have dinner here?" Perry said.

Henry texted and got an affirmative reply.

After the boys had stuffed themselves with Lisa Normal's legendary spaghetti and meat sauce, they went back to work in Perry's room.

 Before long Henry was on his feet.

"Perry! Perry! Did you know that Fort Stanwix had another name? It was also called Fort Schuyler during the War. How come my name comes up over and over in this historical period? What if they *all* are my relatives and ancestors? What *if*, Perry?"

"You never know, Henry!" Perry was grinning. They were both grinning.

***

"We don't keep records going back that far," said the lady on the phone. She was the archives director for The National Personnel Records Center in St. Louis. "Sorry, young man. Maybe try the National Archives in College Park, Maryland. Their number is 1-800-877-2000. Good luck."

The phone clicked and Henry hung up.

"What was the last known address of your relative?" The voice seemed helpful.

"Ah, well, they ah…last lived in, like, upstate New York somewhere near the Hudson River in 1777."

The voice coughed. "Did you say '1777'?"

"Well, he was a famous soldier and officer, and somebody somewhere must have a record of what happened to him or who his family was…".

Henry's voice trailed away.

"Unfortunately, our archives only go back to the Civil War in 1861. The Revolutionary War happened when the United States didn't even exist, strictly speaking. Have you tried the State repository in Albany? They sometimes have old documents that go way back to colonial times. Can you find the number yourself, and do you want me to look it up for you?"

"That's okay." Henry put the phone down. "What now?" He looked over at Perry.

"Henry, I'm going back to the DNA thing. Police find murderers dozens of years later using DNA analysis and genetic matching. There must be something that someone somewhere has in their possession that has been in the hands of, or on the back of, Major-General Philip Schuyler, one of the top officers in George Washington's army. There *has to be!* If we only knew where to look for it!

Bob Caygeon was *trying* to help.

"Look, Henry. How about I call my contact in New York City at The Genealogical & Biographical Society on West 44th Street. They have an impressive database, and a girl I went to Columbia with is chief of records. If anyone knows, she will know."

"Could you do that? I mean, what if they have some artifacts or something?" Henry was all ears.

"Well I can try to find out, and if they don't, who *would* have something of interest for us. They also keep a list of private collectors who have hoards of old stuff from guns, to uniforms, even shoes worn by soldiers and civilians.

I will get back to you as soon as I can, Henry."

"Thank you, Mr. Caygeon. I can't stop this now….I just *have to* know!" Henry shook Mr. Caygeon's hand and closed the door firmly behind him.

Destiny was tracking down Henry G. Schuyler of Brackendale, New York. But what came next, no one could guess.

***

"Oh really? Carla could you fax me that?" Bob Caygeon was speaking with his contact in New York.

"I have a bigger favor to ask. Is there *any* way a DNA sample could be taken *from the sword itself*—say, from the hilt? There might be blood, sweat, or skin cells from its owner embedded in the grip or pommel. Our museum here will cover the cost of the analysis. I know you have a lab that does incredible work. It's kind of important and it affects a family living right here in Brackendale.

Thanks so much, Carla. Be in touch. Bye."

Henry's cell chimed.

"Henry? It's Bob Caygeon from the museum calling. Listen, I have an idea. Could you and Perry come down later today? I think you might like this. Okay, great. See you then."

"It struck me in the middle of the night. I couldn't sleep after that," Bob began.

"What if we could get a DNA specimen from the general's sword that would likely be genuine, and send that to a lab to get the genome or gene readout? We just might have the first DNA proven to be from the Revolutionary War!

We *know* the sword is his, and we assume no one but General Schuyler ever owned it since it was retrieved from his study when he passed away. It has been held in a government vault, along with other memorabilia, so the public has never seen this sword, let alone touched it.

If we can get an uncontaminated sample of *his* DNA we could then test *your* DNA and see if there is a match-- or at least a correspondence that would suggest he may be your ancestor."

Henry got up so quickly he kicked over his chair.

"Are you serious, Mr. Caygeon? Could they really prove that?"

Perry asked: "How will you get a specimen of Henry's DNA to test against the sample from the sword?"

Bob Caygeon opened his filing cabinet and removed a small plastic kit. Inside there were small vials with labels, cotton swabs in sealed packages, a small bottle of isopropyl alcohol and cotton swabs.

"Come here, Henry. You're not afraid of blood are you?"

"Not if you don't make me bleed a lot. You won't will you?" Henry looked apprehensive.

"No, just a prick, and the pipette holds the drop of blood and I place it into the sterile vial. I take the long stick and poke your cheek for saliva, place that one in a sterile tube and seal it and we're done. I will courier it to New York by 5 pm today."

"When will we know?" Henry started to pace the floor and babble, as he always does when he is either super excited or somewhat nervous, or both.

"Depends on the lab in the city. Shouldn't be more than a week. That depends of course on how soon my contact Carla can get the sword sample to them, so thcy have something to compare."

Henry and Perry biked to The Malt Shop. They rushed inside and spilled the whole story to the gang.

"Are you serious?" exclaimed Charmaine and Rita in one voice.

"I can't believe I may be a direct descendant of a famous general in American history—in New York history!" Robert and Perry squeezed together on the bench, and Max drew up a chair.

"That is beyond awesome," Max said. Robert nodded vigorously, then ordered more fries and gravy for everyone.

"I don't mean to be a wet blanket," Robert said between mouthfuls, "...but what if there is no match? Or they can't get a decent sample from the sword itself? Just saying...".

"I think they can—and they will," Perry said. Everyone respected Perry even more than their teachers because he was beyond smart and knew more than almost anyone.

"We just have to wait and see," he said.

Rita spoke up now. "What if you *are*, Henry, and General Schuyler hid an enormous treasure or something, and you are legally entitled to recover it?

All the others in the family line may be dead by now, and only you are left alive to inherit it all!"

That started a wild discussion that Miss Floon, the librarian at Brackendale Middle School, liked to call 'pandemonium'.

"No, Henry," said Max. "Your dad is before you, so he will get it."

"His dad will share it, stupid," opined Robert.

"What if they trace the genetic link to some other guy named Schuyler, who lives in some dinky little town somewhere. There's no guarantee it will go to Henry," Charmaine was saying, waving her hands as if that would make it easier to get heard in all the excitement.

"This will end up in court," said Max glumly.

"My dad's an attorney, remember? And a pretty good one. We can ask his opinion on this," Robert said.

Henry's face was flushed pink, and he ran his fingers through his hair several times.

Rita noticed that gravy from his fingers was getting in his hair and wiped his hand with a napkin, gently scolding him.

"What if there's a treasure, Perry? I'll share it with you."

"Thanks, Henry, but let's find it first. My Gramps used to say 'Don't count your chickens till they're hatched'.

"I miss him, Perry. He was a nice man."

For a moment, Perry looked far away as if he were staring at the horizon.

"Yeah, Henry. Me too."

"Okay gang, so let's have a Halloween like never before. There's a party in the cafeteria at lunch, and Charmaine and Rita—oh...Margot too?—are going trick-or-treating tomorrow night. I heard that Principal Adams might give us the afternoon off so let's make the most of it!" Perry shadows had passed.

Perry slid into his jacket and everyone paid up at the cash and tumbled out the front door of the diner. An unearthly full moon rose in the trees as each of them pedaled for home, and its comfort and safety.

Major-General Benedict Arnold was in command of over 700 Continental Army regulars, but hoping to raise another thousand from Major-General Schuyler's forces on the Hudson near Peekskill.

Both Arnold and Schuyler were in agreement about one thing: St. Leger's drive to capture Ft. Stanwix and push east to the Hudson must not be allowed to succeed.

News that General Johnny Burgoyne had left Montreal and was marching his huge army south and would surely re-take Fort Ticonderoga, the most magnificent fort ever built in North America. If St. Leger closed ranks with his forces, it would drive the Continentals out of New York and northern New England—a disaster for George Washington-- and the Revolution!

The council of war was meeting; it was the morning of August 12, 1777, another hot and humid day with rain on and off.

"With respect, General, but I think we can hardly be expected to support Col. Gansevoort at Ft. Stanwix at this time."

One of the older residents of this part of the country was speaking on behalf of his own town and for others in local communities.

Yet all of New York was ablaze with battle and preparations for battle. Sons and brothers were pulled from farms and mills to enlist in the fight for Independence. Many felt that the Congress in Philadelphia had gone too far by attacking the British, who now were crushing the American patriots in New York City and the Hudson Valley.

Major-General Philip Schuyler arose and spoke directly to the council of civilians and military officers.

"If you hope to save your homes and towns, that time is past. Since July of last year when Jefferson published The Declaration of Independence, we Americans have been at war. The King has one goal: to destroy the movement and defeat our army. Let me quote Patrick Henry, who expresses my own sentiments exactly: 'Give me Liberty, or give me Death!'"

The council erupted with comments for and against the general's emotional statement.

"We cannot allow Col. Gansevoort to stand alone and face an onslaught from the British general St. Leger and his Iroquois braves," he continued.

At that very moment, before Gen. Schuyler could go on, the doors burst open and a very dirty and tired Lt.-Col. Marinus Willett staggered into the room and fell into a chair. All conversation grew silent.

Willett stood and saluted his general, then slumped back in his chair, calling for water. His story changed everything as it tumbled from his lips.

"Sir! I have been three days in the woods, through the swamps, harassed by natives; I bring news! Fort Stanwix is under siege from British soldiers and their Indian allies. We have almost nothing to eat, and only as much ammunition as a man can carry in his own pockets. We implore this council to come to our aid without delay!"

 Benedict Arnold, an equally high-ranking Continental Army officer called for whisky, and poured a stiff glass for Lt.-Col. Willett.

Bolstered by the liquor, Willett went on.

"Have you heard what happened at Oriskany?"

Schuyler nodded.

"We hurt them, but they hurt us worse. Even as I speak, St. Leger is circling the fort with artillery, demanding surrender. Col. Gansevoort has refused— three times! He has dispatched us under cover of night to seek reinforcements."

Willett emptied the glass of whisky and motioned for more. An orderly filled his glass to the brim, and Willett's shaky hands splashed some on his filthy uniform.

"I will lead the men, sir." Arnold was now on his feet, hands behind his back in a way that suggested that he was a man of decision, a man that knew how to lead.

"Very well, Gen. Arnold. March to Ft. Dayton, see what men you can enlist into service. From there, go west up the Mohawk to Ft. Stanwix-- and give 'em hell!"

General Schuyler's eyes were fierce and determined but General Arnold's were orbs of fire! The Dark Eagle was about to fly into the western sun with battle and vengeance on his mind!

***

General Arnold soon arrived at Ft. Dayton with 700 regular soldiers, accompanied by Willett. Their goal was to convince local friendly Oneida and Tuscarora Indians to join their ranks and support their cause against the British. Not all native peoples sided with the Mohawks and Seneca Nations—some trusted the Americans, and opposed their traditional tribal enemies. It was difficult for anyone to know whom to trust.

Arnold, however, was not successful in gathering the men he needed. The small landowners and pioneers lacked experience in battle—they were farmers, better acquainted with horse and plow, than ball and musket.

Willett was desperate—perhaps Ft. Stanwix had already succumbed to the siege. Perhaps a British flag flew over the ramparts already.

Arnold was a bold man. Men looked up to him and would follow him into the heat of battle or the grueling march through forests and swamps. They waited on his decision.

"Col. Willett, will you sit down and stop pacing the blasted floor! You are making me nervous. Sit, and steady your nerves. Here, have a glass of that whisky of mine that you enjoyed so much on the day you arrived.

Now, listen, man, and I will spin you a clever plan that just might do the trick.”

General Arnold explained his ‘clever plan’ over the next twenty-five minutes while Willett slugged back several shots of potent homemade whisky.

“We need to send some of the Loyalists we have captured from this area to Stanwix, to St. Leger himself. And we will tell them to tell Gen. St. Leger that many thousands of Continental Army troops are advancing from the east, coming to break the siege at the fort.

Maybe, just *maybe*, he will buy it --and believing he cannot continue his campaign to sweep the Mohawk valley, capture Ft. Stanwix, and force the patriots to surrender, he will react the way I hope he will react.”

“Which is what, sir?”

“Which is retreat, Willett, run for his life back to Canada! I hope he will regret having gotten himself into this whole mess. Of course, it has to do with Johnny Burgoyne and his grand scheme to conquer New York in the first place.”

"But Burgoyne's plan is a good one, pardon for saying that, sir. They have seized Ticonderoga. They are moving south toward Saratoga. Do you honestly think if we stop St. Leger it will impact the outcome of the War?"

"That's why George Washington placed me in command. If Gen. Gates would see me as his equal, we could accomplish much. We don't have time to waste, Willett. Let's make this happen!"

The two officers were fortunate in finding a Loyalist who knew these woods well and happened to know the Mohawk language well enough to communicate with Joseph Brant's Iroquois.

Gen. Arnold stood at the edge of the dark forest, and told them one last time:

"Don't stop, don't quarrel with any natives you meet, and tell Brant that Dark Eagle comes with many warriors and will surely bring Death with him. Tell him that. In the Mohawk tongue, of course.

And then tell St. Leger that you—Hon Yost-- escaped for the sole purpose of warning him that Arnold and several regiments of the Continental Army are even now pushing west to drive him out.

Make it convincing. Start running! Nightfall is coming!"

Soon the footsteps of Arnold's messengers could no longer be heard, and he returned to quarters to have a hot meal, something he rarely got in these days of conflict and danger.

***

It was August the 23rd and the dawn light filled the courtyard as Gen. Arnold and three hundred foot soldiers prepared to go west to liberate Ft. Stanwix and hold it for the American forces.

   "No idle chatter, aim to be stealthy as we approach. This will be ten miles you will not forget. I cannot promise you anything but toil and danger. But I will stand with you to face whatever Providence has in mind for us. Ready? March!"

The men snaked along the riverbank, following trails animals had worn into the earth as they came to drink the water and travel through the woods. Footprints of deer were pressed into the soft soil, but these men were not hunters, even though a tasty dinner of roast venison would have given much pleasure to their growling bellies.

Mile after mile they slipped through bush and over low ridges, drawing ever near to their destination.

Arnold was expecting to hear noise or laughter or something from the enemy, as sounds carry far in the still morning air, but—nothing. It was too quiet.

He sent an Oneida scout to run ahead and reconnoiter the fort. He brought back strange news.

"Gate open, Dark Eagle. No redcoats there. No Mohawk either. Only smoke from small fires with white men who eat. They no see me."

"That may be the best news I've heard in months," said Gen. Arnold with a smile. "Hear that Willett? "

It was the next afternoon before Arnold and Willett's contingent arrived at Ft. Stanwix.

"Who are you?" asked Gen. Arnold of the men seated round the fire.

"Give us pipe tobacco, sir, and we shall tell you."

"Cheeky lad, I could have you hanged, but I won't. Where is the British commander? Where are his soldiers? Where is Gansevoort?"

Filling their pipes with smiles and nods of gratitude, the young man dressed in blue breeches seemed willing to speak.

"You're too late to bid Gen. St. Leger farewell, sir. They fled west to Lake Oneida some hours ago. Left behind most of everything—except tobacco and rum, which is what we really need right now."

"Who is in command here? I expected a siege and I got a siesta." Arnold dismounted and had one of the men led his horse away to be brushed and fed.

"Col. Gansevoort is, sir. However, he's taken ill with fever, and lies upstairs in his bunk. We are in a bad way, but with the redcoats leaving, we got to tear open their supplies and find something to eat. Many men are suffering from scurvy and hunger, those that ain't been shot."

The man's shirt was black with soot and sweat, and he looked like he needed a good meal, or maybe a bath.

"At ease, soldier. I am General Arnold and I am in charge now.

I want thirty of my men who are willing, and twenty braves from the Oneida, to push west on the trail of St. Leger. If you find them, harass them. I need to know that the British will not return to Ft. Stanwix. Who will go?"

The marvelous thing about native Indians is their endurance and stamina. They move swiftly through the woods like deer do, and the regulars had trouble keeping up.

Inside of two hours, they arrived at the shore of Lake Oneida. To their surprise, the last of the boats had pushed off, and although they fired several rounds at them, the Americans could only watch as the men in red slipped into the mist and darkness, never to return to American soil.

Fort Stanwix would never fall to the British, and Johnny Burgoyne would lose his offensive at Saratoga where three thousand redcoats would surrender to Benedict Arnold and Horatio Gates. It was the beginning of the end for British rule in the Thirteen Colonies that would soon become the United States of America.

PART II   WHERE IT MAY LEAD

CHAPTER SEVEN   MEMORIAL DAY

Every year many towns in America remember the fallen soldiers of many wars by having a Memorial Day event—such as a parade, or marching bands, or a festival of some kind. Brackendale was no different. Located in a cozy little corner of upper New York in the Finger Lakes region, Brackendale was a perfect example of a small town, so small it did not have a high school or a stadium or a shopping mall.

It was a quiet mainly residential location without traffic, or crime, or any of those nasty things that come with being urban. If you wanted urban, Rochester was forty-five minutes drive to the north.

There were less than eight thousand souls here. Many worked from home using Internet, running small businesses. Other local entrepreneurs had stores and shops that had a small-town feel that came with being a smaller community. Many were retired.

The town council decided this year would be dedicated to remembering the heroes of the American Revolutionary War who fought the British near the Hudson Valley. They trouble was—they couldn't decide just how to celebrate this proud part of New York history. Should they have a parade? A display at the Museum of American History—one of the tourist draws of their town?

So they turned to the community. They had a poll where people had three choices and could vote by phone or online, or even dropping by Town Council and filling in a form. Of course, this had to happen in September so planning for November could begin.

The Principal at Brackendale Middle School proposed a dramatic re-enactment of the British defeat at Saratoga—on a small scale, of course, with the school's Drama Club taking the lead. It was decided that all the teachers would assist, and that certain students would play the important roles.

Town Council heartily approved this proposal since it took the responsibility from their shoulders for a Memorial Day event—they even contributed several thousand dollars toward paying for costumes, props, and so on.

"I think I would like to play the part of Major-General Philip Schuyler," Henry announced at the first meeting. "My family name is the same as his, and who knows? Maybe he is a distant relation."

Joanne Van Pelt was the new head of Dramatic Arts at Brackendale. Her background in Theatre and Performance made her a valuable addition to the school. She had even won awards.

"Okay Henry. Now who should play General Benedict Arnold? Someone who can act like a leader."

"Perry Normal!" several kids shouted. "Yes! Per-ry, Per-ry!" the whole room chanted, so Mrs. Van Pelt turned to Perry.

"You have some fans here, Perry. How about it?"

"Can I use what I know about the War and work it into the script? Not too far from here is the historic site of Fort Stanwix. Arnold was involved."

Joanne Van Pelt laughed softly and said: "Of course. Let's make it real, people. Let's study our characters and the story of what really happened. We owe it to history, and we owe it to Brackendale!"

Loud cheering broke out and the excitement was building.

Since she was new, Mrs. Van Pelt did not know Randy the Gorilla at all. But he was big and strong and had kind of a wild look on his face half the time, so she fingered him for the part of Gen. Gates.

"Me?" said Randy in astonishment. "You want me to play an army commander? What if I fuck it up? Ah, sorry Miss, I mean 'mess up'. I don't know much about acting."

"That's fine, Randy. We'll coach you. There will be a short script that you can memorize, or even read aloud during the play if you have to. We're not heading to the stage in New York City or anything."

Perhaps it was her gentle ways that brought the whole thing together, but by November they were ready.

She had worked closely with all of them—especially Randy—and turned a small group of middle-school students into actors in a matter of seven weeks.

Miss Floon even came to rehearsals and gave little five-minute talks about the history and geography.

Mrs. Busby—the English teacher—had given the students writing assignments that required some historical research into their characters.

"This is cool!" said Max, who was playing Gen. John Burgoyne, the dashing British commander. "We get credit in English for doing stuff for the play."

Since there were no prominent female participants in the War, the girls helped make costumes, fit wigs on the boys, and do their makeup—which made some of them, like Randy, very antsy.

"You put this goop on your face every day?" he complained to Rita.

"Hides the acne, silly. Or in your case, giant zits on your chin," she teased. "Hold still, you big...gorilla..."

Suddenly, it was performance day. They had taken over the gymnasium in the community center, the same one that served as a refuge in the big storm and blackout of last year.

That was the time that Max got to help make food in the back kitchen for dozens of locals without power or heat. And Perry and Henry and the girls helped pass out blankets and toys. No one in town would forget that storm anytime soon.

The gym had a decent-sized stage, and even spotlights. The curtains were drawn as the students set up props and furniture for the first scene. The audience filed in and every folding chair was occupied. Kids even sat on tables or in aisles.

The place was totally packed and noisy as a school assembly. Of course, most of the students at

Brackendale were there with family and friends. The mayor and town council got two sofas dragged in near the front and were pouring some kind of liquid into their coffee mugs.

The lights went down and the curtains opened. Mrs. Van Pelt gave the introduction and then the first circle of light shone on the front stage.

Into that circle stepped a person with a splendid blue waistcoat, with white shirtsleeves ruffled at the wrist. On his head was a black three-cornered hat and his right hand rested casually on the pommel of his gleaming sword, strapped to his side.

Henry spoke.

   "It is both a tragedy and a triumph that our nation should find itself in a struggle for Liberty," he boomed.

 Each actor had a lavalier microphone so it was not really necessary to speak loudly. But Henry could be heard easily at the far back of the hall.

   "Such is the course of Destiny for our young nation," he continued. "It is to this that I was called."

Everyone was so impressed that they burst out clapping loudly—even though they knew they weren't supposed to clap until the end.

Then another small circle of light shone and Perry dressed in a similar uniform, stepped onto the stage.

"Greetings, General Schuyler. I bear good news about the campaign at Fort Stanwix."

"Indeed, General Arnold. Give it to me at once." Henry was still booming, like he really was a commissioned officer speaking.

"My men have repulsed the attack of the British and their Iroquois allies, and the whole of the Mohawk River valley now belongs to the American people."

Perry tried his best to sound like Henry but he didn't quite make it. One small boy near the front jumped to his feet and clapped like mad when Perry said '....now belongs to the American people'-- which made the audience giggle.

"I salute you, General Arnold. General Washington was right to put his trust in you to drive back our colonial forces—I dare not call them enemy, and yet I detest what their King has forced them to do."

"I fear, General Schuyler, that the bigger struggle lies before us. Come, let us discuss how to meet General Burgoyne as he moves his troops south to Saratoga."

So Perry and Henry exited stage left, the lights went down, and the curtain closed. Now everyone could clap—and they did until their hands hurt.

Second scene. Horatio Gates meets Arnold at Washington's request.

"General Arnold, I presume?" Randy stepped into the center stage spotlight and the audience gasped.

 He looked magnificent in his uniform, his black leather shoes with buckles gleaming, his head held proudly and his height of over six feet quite apparent and quite appealing to the young ladies of the audience.

"Why have you been sent, sir? Does General Washington think we here are not equal to the task? Surely there is no need for *two* commanders in the New York campaign. What do you propose?"

Perry used the elocution skills he had perfected over the years in school debates. He sounded vaguely threatening like a bear does when defending its cubs.

Randy strode across the stage to where Perry was standing and the audience held its breath.

"I agree, General Arnold. There can be only *one*. Tomorrow we will both fight the Redcoats and their savages and see who is the better man. Good day, *General* Arnold."

Randy sneered when he said that and did it so convincingly that Perry actually blushed, although no one in the audience could see it.

The curtains closed around them and a brief intermission was held, mostly to allow families to visit the washroom, or get a hot coffee at the back.

When they were seated again, the curtains parted once more and the scene was outdoors as there were fake trees, and a giant painted mural hung at the back of the stage that depicted hills and a distant lake or river--it was hard to tell.

Standing center stage was Max—wearing a white wig and a jolly red waistcoat and white leggings and a bunch of lace or fabric at his throat. He also wore a black tricorne hat with a Union Jack sewn onto the front of it.

He was extending his sword laid flat across both of his hands into the darkness. The audience was puzzled. Who is this guy and why is he holding his sword that way?

Out of the shadows stepped Randy---General Horatio Gates, who looked very ferocious at this precise moment.

"You have fought bravely, General Burgoyne, but we have shown you our resolve and our cannon. Your defeat and the surrender of your large regiment is the just reward of those who oppose Liberty and Justice.

I will not take your sword; take it back to England and tell your King that America belongs to its people and their glorious belief in the rights and freedoms they fight for."

Max bowed deeply and left the stage. Perry came onstage and stood beside big Mike.

"Your strategy was impressive, General Gates. I salute you."

"And I—you, General Arnold. I have to say that you and your men distinguished themselves on the field of battle today. This is a great victory for the American cause."

"For the cause of Liberty, sir, for which we strive and struggle," said Perry.

"Shall we now celebrate our victory in a manner befitting gentlemen?" said Randy, fully in tune with his character. "For now we can forget that we are soldiers, even if for only one night, and behave as men."

"Yes indeed, Horatio. Perhaps even as comrades who will henceforth consider themselves 'friends'".

And so the curtains slowly closed, and the two boys walked backstage arm in arm to thunderous applause.

CHAPTER EIGHT   A GHOST AWAKENS

It was close to midnight when families finally put their lights out and their children to bed. It had been an entertaining show at the community hall. A bit of Old New York history.

The mayor himself was fast asleep and perhaps snoring like he briefly did on the sofa at the front of the hall--to his wife's embarrassment but to the townspeople's amusement.

So no one could explain how or why the town bell in the tower rang three distinct times at exactly twelve. Bong! Bong! Bong!

It startled those who heard it—it normally rang on important dates such as Christmas or New Year's. But on Memorial Day? Not in living memory said the oldtimers the next day in the tavern. No, sir-ee!

There were strange lights seen in the woods. There was a light or a lantern seen on Lantern Bridge by folks returning to town from down Syracuse way, sometime after twelve, they said.

Various people reported noises like stones being thrown or loud bangs here and there. Some kids walking from Tesla Park said they heard cries or groaning coming from the woods behind them.

They wondered if their parents even needed to know. Who would believe them anyway?

The old mansion on the rise at the edge of town was unoccupied since it was put up for sale over a year ago. But some folks swear there were lights upstairs this night, and figures seen behind the shades.

They even saw smoke and cinders rising from the brick chimney but no one dared approach to see if any of it were true. Most people are superstitious and don't go out in the night anyhow. Only bats and owls do that, they said.

***

Principal Adams poked his head inside Mrs. Busby's English class in Room 102.

"I just want to say how much we enjoyed your skit last night, Perry and Henry."

'Skit' was the kind of word people used when they weren't sure what to call a short performance.

"Hey, what about *me*, Mr. Adams?" Randy waved from the back corner of the class where he usually sat.

Oh—and you too, Randall. Very impressive. Thanks to all of you for making our school proud with your efforts." And his head just disappeared and the door closed quietly.

"Why does he always have to call me 'Randall'?" Randy said. "Just because the attendance roll gives my full name doesn't give anyone the right to call me by it. Only my Gran called me Randall, but she's dead."

And so far as Randy the Gorilla was concerned, that was the end of it.

Mrs. Busby said we would start our study of longer poems with Alfred Noyes' classic *The Highwayman*.

The poem was quite spooky, to begin with.

"The wind was a torrent of darkness among the gusty trees..." she began, reading aloud—as she always did.

" The moon was a ghostly galleon tossed upon cloudy seas...". The word 'ghostly' hit a nerve with all those students-including Henry and Perry-who were witnesses to last night's strange happenings around their little town. 'Poltergeists' was the word Perry used.

"The road was a ribbon of moonlight over the purple moor...". The imagery used the visual senses, said Mrs. Busby. They evoke mental pictures, she said.

What she didn't say is that the poem also evoked emotions, like--scary ones.

Worst of all, the poem is about a handsome rogue who gets killed and his ghost returns to haunt the old inn where his lover lived.

When class was over, everyone rushed the door to get out into a familiar place—the hall full of laughing, shoving kids.

Perry and the gang naturally gravitated to their 'home away from home': The Malt Shop. Many happy hours were spent chatting and complaining and, of course, stuffing themselves at The Malt Shop. Robert once told the owner Dave and his wife—half-jokingly- that they should build an addition on the back with bunkbeds so the gang could just sleep over and be there for breakfast in the morning.

"That poem is creepy," said Margot.

"I know, eh," said Rita.

"Perry? What have you found out about the stories going around about ghosts, or *a* ghost? I mean, since the Memorial Day festivity there has been some kind of strange mood in this town. Agreed?"

"Well, Rita, has it occurred to anyone that spirits of the Dead might be awakened? Assuming the Dead *are* spirits, and assuming that long-ago soldiers might still be....lurking? hanging? no...wait...

...appearing...just to give the Living a message or something."

"You best not say 'hanging' Perry," Robert said. "You know, some of those guys maybe got hanged by the British, or whatever."

"Let's not make this any more weird than it already is, people," said Charmaine. "Remember—we already have a ghost at Lantern Bridge. That girl—remember?"

"I almost forgot," Margot said. "That was...what... August, when we were last out there?"

"I mean is there something we are not looking at?" said Charmaine.

"You mean the legitimate presence of a genuine spirit from the other world?" Margot stated the obvious.

"Yes. That and all this poltergeist activity recently," Charmaine replied.

"Oh man, is this, like, zombie apocalypse?" Robert said.

"Hey...zombies are potentially real, too," said Max.

"Let's focus on one monster at a time, okay Robert?" said Charmaine sounding exasperated.

"You said we should try to help that ghost...ah, girl..." said Rita.

"I think we need to spend more time at Lantern Bridge."

The group got rather quiet all of a sudden.

"I might be able to get my Dad's car," said Mike.

"You don't even have a driver's license," said Randy.

"Well, how we gonna get out there? Too far to walk."

Robert said, "No worries. We'll take a taxi like last time we went to that other haunted bridge—the one with no name. I'll pay for it."

"I forgot!" said Charmaine. "Geez, all we do around here is chase ghosts. Maybe we should take up bowling or something."

Henry's cell buzzed.

"That was Mr. Caygeon. He says he has some information for me. Who wants to go with me to the Museum?"

"The museum. How boring can you get?" Mike said.

"Don't be mean, Mike. Henry and Perry have something going with the museum and sooner or later, it will result in an adventure for the rest of us-- who have no lives!"

Max was sticking up for Henry, but everyone knew there was a grain of truth in what he said: Perry and Henry had the most extraordinary adventures.

"I'm coming," said Max.

"Me too," said Rita.

"I've got homework," said Margot.

"I've gotta work on my motorcycle," said Randy, "and Mike's gotta help me."

***

When Henry arrived with his friends, the door was locked, so he rang the funny clapper bell that was attached to the side jamb. An antique, like everything in this museum.

"Come in, come in," said Mr. Caygeon. "Pardon the mess, I never have time to clean up." There were tools and wood shavings and strange looking instruments that they used in the 1800s but nobody knows what they're for now.

Mr. Caygeon self-consciously swept his hair back, revealing a swatch of silver at the temples. He had been managing this museum for as long as anyone could remember.

"I have some amazing news, Henry. Are you comfortable sharing it with your friends here?"

"Sure. My friends are like my own family. I don't hide anything from them."

"Good. Well, you remember some weeks back we sent the DNA sample to New York to be compared to the sample they hoped to get from General Schuyler's personal sword?

Well, they got the results and e-mailed them to me this morning. Henry—you won't believe this, but you have a *direct genetic link* with Major-General Philip

Schuyler of the Continental Army of New York. He is your great-great-great grandfather it seems.”

“Are you kidding?” Max and Rita leaped to their feet.

“Are you sure?” Perry said. “I don’t want you to give Henry any misapprehension here. He takes this very very seriously.”

“Here. I printed it out. 99% level of confidence that there is a genetic match, with odds of less than one in twelve million that it is wrong.”

I don’t believe what I’m hearing,” Henry said. He was dumbfounded.

“You are related to the very war hero you portrayed on stage a couple of weeks ago, Henry!”

 Max was going full-tilt. “How cool is that?! Like, what are the odds?”

“I think we should insert a piece in the *Courier* about you, Henry. I’m sure everybody in town would love to know. Naturally, you will have to tell your parents first, and get their consent and all that.”

Bob Caygeon seemed as excited as the rest of them.

For the rest of the way home, his friend teased and praised him by turns, calling him 'General Schuyler' and stuff like that.

For Henry, it was like a birthday--to the eighth power!

Everyone knows the famous tale of The Headless Horseman of Sleepy Hollow. But how many know it is based on a real story from the American Revolutionary War? This was what Perry wondered.

The gang was sitting in The Malt Shop having a late breakfast on a Sunday morning. It was November and Thanksgiving was coming.

"Was The Headless Horseman real?" asked Margot.

"Yes," Perry replied. "In fact, he was a Hessian mercenary hired by the King to fight in America. There were hundreds that came across the Atlantic to the Thirteen Colonies."

"What's a Hessian?" asked Margot.

"What's a mercenary?" asked Rita.

"Soldiers for hire from Eastern Germany, which at that time was a loose collection of states—one of which was called Hesse."

Now it was Henry's turn.

"Remember the story of Washington crossing the Delaware? Christmas 1776? He crossed the frozen river with his loyal troops to surprise the 1500 Hessians who were camped on the New Jersey side but like many armies, were taking a break for the holiday."

"What happened then?" said Robert.

"Washington caught them sleeping—literally. He captured hundreds of Hessians and their food and weapons, which ended up being a big help to Washington's starving troops."

"So what about the headless one?" said Robert.

"How does a headless guy ride a horse?" asked Rita.

"He was dead; dead people can do stuff," said Robert giving a little shrug with his left shoulder.

"In this small village in the Catskills way up the Hudson there were skirmishes between loyalists and patriots," Perry continued, "and Hessian troops were involved in 1776 because the British were not winning the war like they thought they would. So they hired European soldiers to fight."

"Only, one of them seemed to have been on the wrong end of an American cannon and it blew his head off," said Max with glee.

"Since that time," Perry said, "an apparition has haunted a particular graveyard in Sleepy Hollow New York, and is seen on certain nights of the year riding up and down a dark stretch of road."

"Man! That is some kind of spooky!" said Max, who liked ghost stories. "That reminds me of the poem *The Highwayman* where the guy gets ambushed by government agents and so his ghost rides on the moor on moonlit nights."

"So why, Max, is there not more popular recognition of ghosts and spirit hauntings? I mean we are trying to figure out the mystery of Lantern Bridge, which is obviously haunted. Is there a definition of 'haunted'?" Margot was curious.

"Ask Perry. He's the expert," Max replied.

"Actually, there are haunted places all over America, including New York. It's common where there has been conflict and violent death…"

"For example," Robert cut in, "the girl at Lantern Bridge. Killed instantly in a car crash. Only she still has her head."

Max punched him playfully in the ribs.

"That's why Charmaine said we gotta help her. She's dead, but there is something she has to do in the world of the living, but she can't—'cause she's dead!"

"Well said, Rita," said Robert. "So how can people who are still alive, still in *this* world, help people in the spirit world?"

"Well start by *believing* in their world," Perry said. "If people deny the possibility of life after death, they won't see things that might be right before their eyes."

"Native people believed in the Two Worlds," said Margot. "They treated ancestors and animal spirits just like ordinary human beings, and prayed to the same God we do."

"So what is God?" said Robert.

"The Indians call him The Great Spirit: Gitchee Manitou in the Algonquin language. God is the Creator, they say, which is what the Bible says anyway, so God is the ultimate spiritual Being I guess you could say."

"I need an extra-large order of fries and gravy if we are going to get deeper into this," Robert said seriously.

"Me too," chirped Henry, who was a huge fan of the diner's amazing food, home-cooked by Dave and his wife Wanda.

"So," Perry continued, "it's easy to see how folklore and fact get tangled, each one lending credibility to the other. There are many tales of haunting that are part fact, part fiction."

At that moment, Charmaine burst in, bringing cold and a few flakes of snow with her.

"You won't believe what my uncle told me!" she blurted out.

"Do tell!" said Rita and Margot at the same time.

"He was coming back from Syracuse after dropping a load of lumber for a construction site that needed two-by-fours and planking..."

"Okay, cut the lumberyard details, what happened?" said Max impatiently.

"So he was coming up on Lantern Bridge when he saw the light, the yellow glow, so he pulled his truck to the shoulder and turned off the motor.

Sure enough, it was a lantern, one of the old kinds, swinging back and forth as if some invisible force were carrying it along the bridge."

"And then? Don't stop!" said Max.

"My uncle is a pretty down-to-earth guy, okay. He owns and runs a lumberyard. He's a businessman."

Max gave her that look of exasperation again, so she continued.

"So he is not one to believe in the paranormal or in hauntings and such. But you could see what he saw scared him when he was telling us about his experience.

He saw the arm and then the coat and then the man—it was a soldier dressed in Continental Army regalia, right down to the white breeches and three-cornered hat.

His face was in shadow so he didn't get to see much of his features. The soldier was hanging the lantern over the railing as if to see something in the water."

"Like he was looking for something?" Rita said.

"Yeah, something like that. My uncle backed away and jumped into his truck. He really didn't know what to do at that moment. So he texted my auntie that he would be home soon, and then sat there and lit a smoke and continued watching the figure on the bridge.

Only, after he rolled down the window to let the smoke out, the soldier was gone and the lantern light with him.

He started the truck and hightailed it home!"

"Isn't it kind of a coincidence," said Margot, "that we have been telling ghost stories and in comes Charmaine with some kind of confirmation, a ghost right here in our town?"

Everyone agreed, and after the fries were done, they slipped into their coats and went home quickly, as the days of November grew ever darker as the year dwindled away.

***

Perry was home on his computer. Henry was chatting with him online.

"Parapsychology is the study and investigation of unusual phenomena such as telepathy, clairvoyance, and awareness of the supernatural." Henry was reading the encyclopedia on his desk.

"So if they use words like 'phenomena' and 'supernatural', aren't they admitting these things are real, they really happen Perry?"

"Good point, Henry. You can't investigate something that doesn't have a tangible reality, even if it is in the Mind. Think about it, Henry.

Ordinary psychology studies the brain and nervous system, studies thinking and memory and reasoning.

The Mind is a marvelous thing because it interprets what we sense and feel about the world around us, then organizes it logically and methodically and stores that information.

We understand the world and can even make predictions about future events. Like who will win the next federal election, or what the trajectory of an incoming comet in relation to the Earth will be."

It is well known in Brackendale that Mr. Perry Normal, Junior Scientist, is fully qualified to have such a title. His IQ is over 175 and his brain holds as much information as a Cray supercomputer—if not more. At least that's what Mr. Matson, the Science teacher says.

"So there is a scientific basis for strange and unusual phenomena, right?" Henry said.

"Exactly. There does not have to be a conflicting viewpoint about the supernatural if we can apply Science to the study of such phenomena—just like we study radio waves and subatomic particles.

We can't see those, not even in a microscope. But we can measure them using instruments, and infer their reality using scientific theory and research to test those theories."

"So are there people with instruments who are investigating ghosts and apparitions and things that apparently slip in and out of our third-dimensional world?"

"*That* is what we need to find out, Henry."

***

"You are not going to believe this, Henry, but there are nearly a hundred paranormal investigation organizations in New York State alone!

Here are some examples: in Tonawanda the group is called 'The Buffalo Boo Crew'. In Jordan, they are called 'The Ghost Hunters Alliance of Central New York'. In Oriskany, their name is 'R.I.P. Activity'".

"I bet *they* have Revolutionary War ghosts aplenty, Perry!" said Henry, speaking with irony.

"There are at least four or five in Rochester, like Rochester Paranormal Researchers who go by the name 'Phantom Finders'," Perry stated.

"So what you are telling me, Perry, is that ordinary sensible human beings spend their spare time actually hunting ghosts and spirits?"

"We need to connect with these people, Henry. They have the tools, the information, the locations we need to be able to put some scientific floor under our personal investigations," Perry said.

"Well let's e-mail those guys in Rochester and see if they have meetings or outings or something," Henry said.

Thank you for your interest in Phantom Finders in Rochester, N. Y. Please sign up for our events at:

Triple W.meetup.com/Rochester-Phantom-Finders

We welcome all sincere seekers!

"There we go, Perry! We can plan a visit before the holiday. Shall I reply on our behalf?"

***

The room was moderately full, but everyone there had an energy, a way of speaking with each other that showed there was real interest in ghosts here.

Serving Rochester, Monroe County, and western New York said the website.

Perry's Dad Robert, who was well aware of Perry's tendency to get into unusual activities, offered to drive the boys to Rochester for this meetup.

Although he was a financial analyst, he had enough imagination to accept that there were things not easily explained out there—and that his son always seemed to hone in on them!

"Welcome everyone! Especially I see some newcomers." Cookie—the coordinator-- looked at Perry, Henry and Robert with a smile.

"Tonight we have a special guest from England who will speak about one of our perennial favorite topics—orbs! Please welcome Colin Andrews!"

"Thank you, Cookie for having me here tonight. I want to start off by saying that orbs are *real phenomena* and have been seen and photographed numerous times. So we have the proof."

The Englishman described cases from both the U.K. and America, and pointed out current beliefs about what they were, and why they were present at places that were considered 'haunted' or as having strange vibrations or energies such as stone circles like Stonehenge.

He also took a few moments to relate orbs to another area of interest in the supernatural that he was considered an expert: crop circles.

Crop circles occurred worldwide, but especially in the English countryside—no one knew why.

Mr. Andrews had endless photos of circles, and quite a few night shots that showed orbs or balls of light appearing in the fields just before a circle was discovered, often by the farmer who grew the grain that contained the fantastic patterns carved right into the standing crop itself.

Perry quietly spoke to Henry: "This is on our list too, Henry. I don't know how or when, but we have to go to England."

The powerpoint showed amazing streaks and globes of light, some like bubbles of faint color rising around and behind the subject. One lady said on camera that she was a Druid priestess; orbs the size of baseballs floated around her head and body. Mr. Andrews said this was not fakery, and was not photoshopped.

The audience was impressed. So was Perry and Henry who chatted all the way home to Brackendale about what they had seen.

"If people can demonstrate that such phenomena are real enough to photograph, or see with infrared settings on digital cameras in both still and video shots, Henry, then we have justification for searching out and finding out about our Lantern Bridge ghosts."

"Yeah. It seems like it's ghosts *plural* now. I can't wait to get out there with the gang. But there's only one problem."

"What's that?"

"How do we know when the ghosts will appear? It's not like they are predictable, like snowstorms."

"*That* answer is our next topic of inquiry, Henry!"

"I imagine you feel very proud, Henry, and so you *should*," said Miss Floon.

Henry had told her the news about the DNA test and confirmation.

"It is who we are—our roots, our ancestry. We humans are pearls on a thread of Time, tied to each other in mysterious ways. It has always been my belief that the study of anthropology and society give us the necessary reference points from which to give meaning to human life and human endeavor."

"That's what she actually said," said Henry to the Malt Shop Gang.

"It's just like her to use words like 'endeavor'," said Robert.

"I like her," said Rita. "I mean, I respect who she is and what she does."

"I agree," said Margot. "She really believes in her work, in setting standards for scholarship and literacy. I know she has helped *me* improve a *lot*."

"Does anybody know if she has ever been married? Or has kids?" Charmaine wanted to know.

"She has a Master degree in Library Science," Robert revealed. "My Dad knows a lawyer that knew her growing up."

"Where is she from?" asked Rita.

"Albany, I think. She went to SUNY and after she graduated, kind of migrated to Brackendale. She's worked here thirty-six years. My Mom told me. She works for the school board, you know," Perry said.

"That means she has been our librarian for more years than my Mom has been alive!" Robert said.

"Doesn't she get bored," Max said. "I mean, spending your whole career filing and cataloguing books and CDs. I go brain-dead just thinking about it."

"If she's not married, maybe she has a secret past that she keeps hidden from everybody!" Charmaine speculated.

"Yeah, a string of lovers that somehow could never please her," said Rita.

"And they all ended up dead!" exulted Max.

"You guys are freakin' crazy," said Randy as he came in with Mike and slouched into a nearby booth.

"Why is nobody eating?" Randy continued.

"Hey! Don't let me interrupt the juicy conversation about Old Floon."

"There must be something in her past that affected where she is today," Rita said.

"She told me that she also had Dutch-American ancestry," Henry said. "When I told her about General Schuyler and the DNA test."

"'Floon' sounds kind of Old Dutch. What if she's related to *you* too, Henry!" Robert teased Henry in a kind of annoying way because he had that sarcastic streak in his personality.

"Hey maybe the old bag has money stashed away and Henry gets to inherit it, as she has no son." Randy was grinning but meant no harm.

"Yeah! Now that we know Henry is the great-great-great grandson of Gen. Schuyler, did we discuss further the possibility that he might qualify to inherit whatever wealth the general might have got in his lifetime?" Mike was into the conversation now.

"If finding my genetic link was hard, finding out whether there's a fortune with my name on it will be *impossible*," Henry said.

"Maybe someone *killed* him for it!" said Max. "Do we know how he died?"

"Officially, old age," said Perry. "Which means pneumonia probably."

Rita said, "Hey! I have a crazy idea! What if we took Miss Floon out for her birthday or something, and asked her about her life in the past, what really is going on."

Rita was looking at Charmaine for some kind of sign of approval. Charmaine looked at Perry.

"Maybe. When's her birthday?" Perry asked.

"Mrs. Busby said in mid-December. She's a Sagittarius," said Margot.

"I don't know," said Charmaine. "She's kind of a private person."

"How about *I* invite her," said Henry. "She might if I asked her."

"Perfect!" said Rita. "Be sure to tell her that we all want to come and celebrate her birthday. See what she says Henry? Okay?"

***

"Well, this *is* a surprise! When Henry approached me I was a bit shy, but then I thought: 'why not?'"

"I hope you like the place we picked, Miss Floon," said Rita. "Well…Margot and I picked."

"I don't cook much myself. I was always kind of a nerd I guess you could say. My mother scolded me and said I had to learn to cook for my future husband. All the girls were raised that way in my generation."

"Italian food is something we all like and the main dish comes with salad, and fresh bread. This is our treat, by the way Miss Floon." Rita saw everyone nod.

"That is very kind. I know ladies are not supposed to tell their age, but this is Number 63 for me!" Miss Floon seemed quite content to share this.

"Wow!" Max said. "Aren't you ever going to retire?"

"Well, one of these days, Max. I am writing a book and I would like to have more time to devote to that."

"What's it about?" Rita said. Rita knew that everyone was thinking it might be about those secret lovers.

"It's about the American Revolution, actually," Miss Floon said.

But she didn't get to say much more about it because delicious steaming plates of pasta and sauce, Caesar salads covered in fresh parmesan cheese all arrived at once.

Nobody needs to tell hungry kids to eat.

To everyone's amusement, when the maître d' came over, he offered Miss Floon a glass of Chianti--the famous red wine of Italy, 'complimentary' for her birthday. And she graciously accepted and guzzled half of it immediately. Mr. Seraglia filled it again.

"I can't remember when I've had a more enjoyable evening everyone. Thank you so much for thinking about your old librarian on her birthday."

Miss Floon then stepped into a waiting taxi. Max held the door for her, then kissed her hand for some strange reason and Miss Floon giggled uncontrollably; maybe it was the wine, and maybe it was the moment. But it was special, everyone agreed.

"English test next week, people," said Perry, who often tutored his pals in their coursework.

"Party-pooper!" said Charmaine. "Night everyone!"

The neon 'OPEN' sign for Seraglia's restaurant switched off. Time to go home.

***

"Henry? Could you drop by the library to talk to Miss Floon, please?"

Henry had a message to report to the office but the school secretary said 'No, you're not in trouble' so he relaxed a bit as she relayed the message.

He knocked at the door behind the circulation desk once the student assistant let him inside the gate that separated the staff area from the student area.

"Come in," the voice said. "Oh it's you, Henry. Yes, come in. I wanted to ask you something."

Henry sat in a red velvet wing chair across from her desk.

"Now that you know you are connected to a real part of New York history, I wanted to ask your opinion about something."

Henry tried to look composed, but his mind was racing. *Secret lovers? Was Rita right?*

"What if you knew—or found out—that you were related to someone in history who was...how shall I say? Unpopular. You would probably be reluctant to disclose that, hmmm?"

Henry was tongue-tied and just nodded lamely.

"You see, Henry, I too am related to a Revolutionary War hero—Benedict Arnold. He was my great-grandmother's grandfather—if you can follow that. Six generations back the great general married a colonial highborn lady and she had some Dutch in her background."

She studied the bare trees outside the window for a moment, then walked back and sat down.

"That is where the 'Floon' comes from. Because of what happened to the general's reputation after the betrayal of George Washington, and the disgrace that sent General Arnold to England, my family has not spoken openly about this for over two hundred years.

"Nobody in New York wanted to have the family name of 'Arnold' so they used 'Floon' instead.

So instead of pride and happy sentiment, I inherited a shameful secret."

She stood suddenly and looked directly into Henry's eyes.

"I want to change all that, and I want you and Perry to help me!"

Now Henry stood up, fidgety and confused.

"We will do what we can, Miss Floon. Only...we're just Eighth Graders. What do you think we can do to help *you*?"

"Do you know what the word 'exonerate' means?"

"To release someone from guilt or blame."

"Correct. I am going to finish my book about Benedict Arnold and exonerate him—to the extent I can—for the shame Americans have heaped on him. I do this so I feel that I can hold my head up high—as you are now able to do—and tell the true story of my American ancestors.

Promise me you will help, Henry!"

Chapter Eleven   Wolf Skin's Story

"She said that, Henry?"

"I swear, Perry. She has no reason to lie. What do we do next?"

"We keep it under our hats, and we work out a plan with her."

Henry waited for the other shoe to fall.

"In order to change the public perception about Benedict Arnold we are going to have to go over his entire life with a fine-toothed comb.

We need to find every bit of evidence that shows that he was an honorable man, a fine soldier, and a genuine hero—despite his unfortunate mistake.

After all, that mistake did not cost America the War, or even a substantial loss. But it destroyed his relationship with George Washington, who became our national hero and first president, as you know."

"Hey, Perry. Remember that guy we met at the ghosthunters meetup in Rochester? The Indian guy? I think he said he was Oneida."

"Kind of. What's up?"

"I wonder if he would have any information passed down from *his* people about Benedict Arnold. Ft. Stanwix is in Oneida traditional territory I believe."

"More than that, boys," spoke the tall tan fellow with a handmade moosehide jacket. Fort Stanwix was built on Oneida land in 1758, and my ancestors helped build it."

Tekanatokin agreed to meet them right downtown in Brackendale, and he made the two hour journey down from the northeast, where his reservation was situated.

His battered Ford F-150 stood on the street in front of the diner.

"You can call me 'Wolf Skin'—it's easier to say."

"Honestly, I never met a real Indian before," Henry marveled. "Did you make that cool jacket yourself?"

Wolf Skin grinned, and said "Killed and skinned the moose that kindly offered his backside for it."

"You said in your e-mail Wolf Skin that your family and tribal council had stories that spoke of the Revolutionary War and their role in it," Perry said.

"We have traditions in our folklore—we didn't have writing you know, so everything was passed down orally. But I have some of it I can share, since you are sincerely interested in my people and their role in helping America gain its liberty."

"We sure appreciate anything you can tell us," said Henry. "I myself am a direct descendent of General Philip Schuyler, who was senior commander at Ft. Stanwix."

"So you too, Henry, have stories passed down in your family line," said Wolf Skin.

"Ah, well, DNA stories, actually," admitted Henry.

"In any case," continued Wolf Skin, "the story really goes back to The French & Indian War of the 1750s, when the great Six Nations Confederacy started to fray, I guess you could say. Come apart at the seams. And the Mohawk became our enemy instead of our brothers."

"Our people were called Haudenosaunee—people of the longhouse, referring to our dwellings built a little like a townhouse would be today. We enjoyed a communal existence where housing and food were shared, where elders were respected and whose advice became our guiding principles."

"Pardon me for saying it, Tekanatokin, but you speak like an educated man, and the impression most

Americans have of Indians is that they are poor, alcoholic, and have low levels of literacy," said Perry.

"Wonder who pushed us into poverty and addiction?" Wolf Skin's eyes flashed with resentment.

"Actually, I have a B.A. from SUNY in Business Administration. I hope one day to start my own business."

"Oh my gosh! That's great, Wolf Skin." Henry didn't know what else to say at that moment, so Wolf Skin continued.

"Because of the struggle between France and Britain for dominance in North America, the Six Nations—indeed all native peoples—got pulled into the fight to save their land and culture from the European invaders. It was like Star Wars! Our country was being invaded and taken over by a technologically superior society for their own gain.

So of course we had to fight. The big question in that war was who to side with? Who would respect the Indian? Turns out, both sides did, in their own way. The Six Nations we call the Iroquois felt that the British had stronger military leadership, so that is who we went with.

Nobody at the time, including the British, had any idea that the colonies in America would soon rise up and throw off the British colonial government, and create a new nation. I mean NOBODY."

"So they built Fort Stanwix near Lake Oneida to concentrate British control over the south shore of the Great Lakes?" asked Perry.

 "Yes. You probably know—every Canadian kid knows, and I have cousins in Niagara—that Fort Kingston and later Fort York were the focus of British settlement on the north shore of Lake Ontario."

"Did you know that in the War of 1812, Americans invaded Ontario and burned Fort York? Well, it's Toronto now." Henry was getting into it.

"Yes, I've heard that, but native people were not a part of it. All I know is that the British won that struggle for control, and made a treaty with the Six Nations and colonial settlers then pouring into our area in 1768, called the Boundary Line Treaty. Its purpose was to limit white expansion into the red man's land. Fat lot of good it did; they came anyway."

"So less than ten years later, your people were caught up in another war," said Perry quietly.

"You know what the worst thing was? The worst thing was that the Iroquois Confederacy of Six Nations, that had been functioning for many centuries, fell apart. My people and the neighboring Tuscarora people decided to side with the colonists, the Americans. And that is what put us in opposition to the Mohawk, and Seneca, and so on. So by the time Fort Stanwix was under British siege in August 1777, we were firmly allied with the Continental Army—and your relative, Henry!"

"That is so amazing," said Henry. "I know for a fact that Oneida scouts helped General Arnold defend Ft. Stanwix from the invasion from Canada. That fits my definition of 'hero'!"

"Well, 'heroes' are for the victorious, Henry. Even after the defeat of British forces and the establishment of the republic, Oneida people got the dirty end of the stick, we might say.

Settlers came from Germany and Scandinavia and every kind of place to the fertile lands of the Ohio River and the Hudson Valley and the lakes named after our Six Nations. And a small piece of that remains reserved to our people for their use."

"So where exactly is the Oneida land?" asked Henry.

"You're standing on it," replied Wolf Skin.

Henry and Perry felt humbled by the Indian's words. There was nothing any of them could do to change what history had brought to native culture and society.

"One last question before you go, Wolf Skin."

Perry was facing his Indian friend.

"Why do you call yourself 'Wolf Skin'? Tekanatokin sounds so noble, so brave!"

"When I was a boy, like all native Indian boys, we were trained to hunt, to survive in the wild.

One of the tricks, you might say, that we Oneida used to hunt deer and other game was to disguise ourselves by wearing wolf skins on our naked backs. It was amazing how close to our quarry we could get if we silently glided through the brush or high grass crouched in our wolf skin coverings. Besides, they were warm when the cold wind was blowing."

Wolf Skin shook their hands and went to his truck, wiping a half inch of snow from the window with his hand.

A final wave 'goodbye'—and he was gone.

"What happened to Ft. Stanwix after General Arnold arrived in September of 1777 I wonder," said Henry, fiddling with a toy cannon on Perry's desk.

Henry and Perry were in Perry's room. The lights were off and Perry was laying on the bed with his head propped on his crossed arms. Moonlight shone through the window and touched the floor.

"A more important question that we have not answered Henry is what happened to the guy Arnold sent to deceive the British and why was he able to pull it off?" Perry shifted on the bed to face Henry.

"Do we even know his name?" Perry said.

"You're right, Perry. There's a missing piece here. The official history mentions Arnold and Willett coming to lift the siege, but not why the British had fled—leaving most of their equipment and supplies just half a day before the Americans got there."

"And why didn't the Mohawk guards beat the crap out of him to begin with?" said Perry.

"I wonder whether the museum has some records that might shed light on this for us, Henry."

"Have a look in here," said Mr. Caygeon. "This is off-limits to the public. This is where the really valuable stuff is. These are original documents for the first colonial government in Albany that fell into my hands by accident.

You see, there was a garage sale at a barn not far from town..."

Perry cut him off before he turned this into a lecture.

"This is perfect. Henry, you look in that fat volume with the leather cover over there. Wear the white gloves, please. No oily finger marks permitted.

I'm going to sort through these files which appear to be letters."

"Well, if you boys don't need me, I'm going to Starbucks around the corner. Be back soon. I'm locking the front door so you are stuck here for now."

"Thanks, Mr. Caygeon," said Perry. "Take your time."

Perry knew that he and Henry could easily pass hours lost in their research and musings about the past.

One hour passed; then two.

Perry lifted a crinkled brown sheet from the pile and laid it out under the hanging lamp over the worktable.

"C'mere Henry. Take a look. Is this General Arnold's signature? It says that one Hon Yost Schuyler, a Loyalist, has been sent with instructions to delay or confuse General St. Leger until such time as Arnold and more men can be dispatched to relieve the siege."

"So he knows the siege is threatening the Americans inside the fort," said Henry. "Wait! Did you say 'Schuyler'??"

"He spells his name—he *prints* it; I wonder why. I think he was thinking that if Hon Yost Schuyler pulls it off, headquarters and Gen. Philip Schuyler should give credit to this man, and grant him his freedom. He was a captive at Fort Dayton, apparently."

"Oh...my...gawd," Henry said, his mouth hanging open.

"Close your mouth or you'll swallow a fly, Henry," Perry teased.

"Do you see what this *means*, Perry? Another Schuyler just entered the picture. Another guy I might be related to!!"

"And…he might be the hero that nobody knew!" said Perry. "Without him—Arnold would not have been able to advance, so St. Leger and the British would have overcome the defenses of the fort, and…"

"Exactly! Let's keep looking. We *have* to find more about Hon Yost and what actually happened."

Bob Caygeon peered in the door.

"Any luck in here?"

"Yes sir," said Perry. "We might need your help tracking down an individual named Hon Yost Schuyler who was at Fort Stanwix in August 1777."

"Another Schuyler? That can't be a coincidence," said Mr. Caygeon.

"You know what, I'm going to send you to the local library because they will have more books and comprehensive information. Plus they have a database and computers."

So dinnertime rolled around and the boys found themselves doing what few kids in town would be doing on a Saturday night—chillin' at the library!

***

But Hon Yost Schuyler had no such a time to relax. He was being drilled by his commanding officer-- Benedict Arnold.

"You are under my command and you will follow my instructions to the letter, Private Schuyler. Do I make myself understood?"

"Yes, General. Travel west along the valley, past Oriskany, up to the low rise around Ft. Stanwix and once I encounter the guards or the native scouts, convince them I am not an enemy and that I have news for Gen. St. Leger, the Great White Chief. I don't know how that will translate into Mohawk. I'll do my best, sir."

"Look at it this way, Schuyler. You can either serve a distant King who oppresses the brave patriots of this land we call America, or join with us in our cause and struggle. I want you to think about it and in your heart make the choice. I need you. America needs you. Do what you know to be right."

Hon Yost Schuyler thrust two pistols into his belt, tightened his backpack and saluted the general. From here on out, the fate of Fort Stanwix was in his hands.

***

"What is that, Daddy?"

"Where?"

"There ahead—on the bridge!"

The boy and his sister were in the back seat but could see the lantern and the strangely dressed man standing in the middle of the span.

The father slowed abruptly as there was no other traffic either ahead or behind.

He rolled down his window and pointed his cell phone at the figure.

The flash seemed to alarm the person on the bridge who suddenly stepped back and vanished right there before his eyes.

"Where is he, Daddy? You scared him!"

"I don't know kids. Let's get home. Your mother is waiting supper."

That one image from the man's phone found its way on to Facebook and then on to a million viewer's accounts, including Rita and Margot's shared Facebook page.

"This was posted just yesterday and already had a million views!" said Charmaine, poking a straw down into the chocolate shake.

She was at The Malt Shop diner, as was the custom for all the gang from Brackendale Middle School.

"It was taken by a guy crossing Lantern Bridge," said Margot. "Look closely!"

Max and Rita crowded into the bench across from Margot and Charmaine.

"All I see is an orangey-yellow glow. I can't make out much else," said Max.

"That's just the point, Max," said Margot. The image is a photograph of an actual object seen by the man and his children on a dark road. Get it?

The ghost is *real* and this is *proof* that it—or he— haunts the bridge where people have reported this...phenomenon."

"Gotcha!" said Max. "So we aren't chasing a hallucination!"

"Correct. And as soon as the Christmas break arrives, I think we should pay a little visit to Lantern Bridge!"

***

The sharp snap of a twig brought the sentry face to face with Hon Yost. In the near distance Hon could see his destination in the mist: Fort Stanwix.

"Ohnka thi?" The sentry demanded in Mohawk.

"Ontiaten," said Hon. "A friend."

"Tekwanonweia:tons" said the guard in welcome.

"Nia:wen" said Hon Yost in thanks, bowing and touching foreheads with the native.

"Oh niiawenhatie?" said Hon. "What's going on?"

And so it was that Benjamin Arnold's secret agent Hon Yost Schuyler found a back door into the enemy camp.

***

"My eyes are shot, Perry," said Henry. It was closing time at the library.

"Let's go to The Malt Shop to decompress, " Perry said.

"I'll call my mom and let her know where I am," said Henry.

"Tell her that you are in the middle of a fascinating mystery about the Revolutionary War and you've discovered another possible relative named Schuyler."

Perry rested his hand on Henry's shoulder as Henry's mother answered.

As they tore into the hot beef open-faced sandwiches smothered in Wanda's secret gravy that drove men mad, Perry continued.

"We know that Hon Yost accomplished his mission and that Arnold reclaimed a virtually empty Ft. Stanwix. And we know that Gen. Gansevoort was too sick to defend it anyway.

So am I reading this the wrong way, Henry? I'm telling you that Hon Yost Schuyler was the guy who saved the fort. Gansevoort couldn't have done it. Arnold and Willett were too far away. The Mohawk were in a lousy mood over the way St. Leger was managing the whole shebang and were starting to desert and go back to their villages."

Henry had that look a starving man has when he has been saved at last by a hot meal.

"Eshackly," said Henry swallowing a bite.

"So Hon Yost Schuyler made the best decision of his young life on his lonely mission to bring fake news to the British occupiers. He crossed over, Henry! He decided on that solitary evening that he would stand with—and for—the Americans."

"Well, what happened to him after? We know Arnold left a few men to hold the fort while he marched off to victory at Saratoga."

"That can only mean one thing, Henry" Perry replied.

"That implies Hon Yost remained at his post as an American patriot while the glorious acts of battle and heroism moved to the east and south as the long bitter defeat of the English came to a conclusion."

"Or *not*, Perry. That was a long bitter struggle. I honestly don't know how Washington was able to get the upper hand under the daunting circumstances his army, his nation, faced."

"But we are not done, Henry. Is Hon Yost Schuyler a distant relative of you, of your family? We *must* find out!"

PART III   CLOSE TO HOME

Chapter Thirteen   The Omen

Perry is an avid astronomer and so is Henry. A couple of years back they got into a sticky situation where their skywatching allow them to see things that were...how shall we say? Not official, not for public consumption, somewhat top secret in fact.

Things turned out alright in the end, but it makes the point that curious minds often discover the unknown or hidden, and of course that is just what Science is: the discovery of new laws of the Universe, development of new theories and postulates.

So it should come as no surprise that this December many eyes were on the skies as a bright green comet called 47P/Wirtanen appeared in the south near the constellation Taurus. Skywatchers of every kind trained their scopes and cameras on this visitor.

Everyone in Science class wanted Perry's comments on whether it would hit the Earth, or cover the skies with green dust, maybe full of toxic metals, and so on.

Mr. Matson in Room 204 turned on local TV news.

Comet Wirtanen is expected to have a close shave with Planet Earth this week, the broadcaster said. *Passing at only a distance of five million miles, many doomsayers believe it is an omen of doom and claim that the Bible's last book predicts an Apocalypse will come and usher in the end of the World. Scientists are more practical and wish to study its sudden presence and its long elliptical orbit to determine its trajectory.*

Mr. Matson turned off the news.

"Well, there's where Science and folklore diverge, Class. Superstitious people say it is an 'sign' or 'omen', but those are the old days—before scientists like Kepler could mathematically model how planets and asteroids move in Space. We know comets are like snowballs full of dust and rocks that have been hurtled out from some larger body, and are caught by the gravity of our star and will continue to circle it until they either collide with something, or just lose their kinetic energy and fall into the Sun.

Now let's start our review for the term tests, shall we?"

Moans and groans could be heard as students opened their binders and took out more paper to take more notes than they had planned on doing in class today.

Perry looked over at Henry and winked. Charmaine gave him a dirty look.

Later, after school at The Malt Shop, he asked her why.

"You are Henry are smart. You never sweat about tests and assignments like us normal students. I get so nervous before a test that I eat five times more that I usually do. Wonder why I have a weight problem!"

"First of all, you *don't* have a weight problem. You are a large girl and people can be mean to larger girls. It's not your fault that Nature made you voluptuous and curvy, and...".

"Volup...WHAT?" Charmaine replied. "Where do you get these words?" But she was smiling because she knew they were compliments somehow, and Perry was a loyal friend who supported her no matter what.

"And besides, I will personally help you prep for the test. Don't I always?" Perry teased.

Rita came in and took her place beside Charmaine. Charmaine pointed a fork at Perry.

"He called me names! Volup...something...and curvy."

"What was your point, Perry?" said Rita, coming to Charmaine's defense.

"My point is that she is attractive just the way she is, and should stop beating herself up for something that is a matter of perception, rather than fact."

"I shouldn't have asked," Rita retorted. "Just like a science geek to make a simple answer complicated."

Margot and Max breezed in.

"Shut the door behind you!" shouted Wanda from the kitchen. "Don't your mothers tell you that?"

"Sorry, Wanda. Thanks for the reminder," said Margot, slipping out of her wool coat and scarf and sliding into the seat across from Charmaine.

"So, do I get to eat this burger and fries-- or not?" Charmaine demanded.

"Abso-freakin'-lutely!" shouted Rita. "Dave? Tell Wanda to make another order, and extra gravy on the fries!"

"So, it's almost the holidays. What's everyone doing for Christmas? And when do we hike out to Lantern Bridge?"

The others were kind of hoping Margot would forget that she was planning to go ghost-hunting at the winter break and bring the whole gang.

"Oh, by the way, Katya is coming home for the holidays. That'll be great," said Margot.

"Where is she?" asked Max.

"In a private school in Connecticut. Her parents want her to go to a 'good' school. They plan to keep her there till Twelfth Grade."

"Anyone seen Perry and Henry?" asked Margot.

"Mr. Matson lent them the telescope from the Science Department, so they lugged it home to Henry's deck and are probably glued to it right now," said Max.

"Figures," said Rita. "Who else are we missing?"

"Mike and the Gorilla are in the pool hall. Robert— I'm not sure. So when is this little field trip to the bridge supposed to happen?" Max said.

"Well, I'm thinking we get Christmas out of the way, and that leaves us a good week to do stuff," Margot said. "Charmaine is our den mother so let's ask her to put it together," she went on.

"Me? Ha! Den mother! Like you are baby foxes and Mama Fox is gonna get you in line. Okay, fine. I accept. I will e-mail everyone the date. Bring gloves and hats. We're gonna get six inches of snow over Christmas. Check ya later!"

With Charmaine gone, and the sun setting, the Malt Shop gang filed out into the cold December night in Brackendale, New York.

***

There were eight days until classes started up again. Christmas was over and the gang had shared all the news about who got what for Christmas, so it was time for Charmaine to keep her promise.

Her e-mail brought everyone to Robert's driveway on a chilly Tuesday afternoon under clear skies, waiting for the minivan taxi.

"What if we see *both* of them," Max said. "Both the girl and the soldier? It's possible, you know!"

"It's also possible we may see no-one," said Robert. "It's possible we will freeze our butts off for nothing!"

Rita was blowing on her fingers trying to warm them with her steamy breath. Margot loaned her spare mittens. Rita smiled and nodded in gratitude.

"Lantern Bridge," said Robert to the driver.

There were eight all together: Henry was sick so Katya took his place. Three boys and five girls, bundled up like they were going to the North Pole.

"Hartford Excel Girls Academy is so boring," Katya was saying. "Everybody just stays in their room or goes to the pool. They don't even go off-campus on weekends."

"So what if they want to, you know, meet a guy?" Rita asked.

"Well, of course there are ways that the older juniors and seniors have figured out. Some of them have regular boyfriends in town who pick them up outside the gates after dark," said Katya.

"And if you get caught?" said Charmaine.

"Some serious shit hits the fan," said Katya. "This is one rule you don't want to break—no dating."

"Yeah, an unwanted pregnancy would be really inconvenient for the Headmistress and Admin Team."

"For sure, Charmaine. But I'm a *good* girl," Katya said.

"You're a Brackendale girl and you always will be," said Charmaine.

So with chitchat about school and gossip, they arrived sooner that expected just at twilight. There was a clearing with a rest stop where the taxi pulled in. Robert spoke to him in a low voice and the driver nodded and lit a smoke.

"Okay people, let's do this," said Robert.

It was about a fifty-yard walk to the bridge itself. The snow on County Rd. 13 had not been plowed recently, however, so they trudged through ankle-deep snow to get there.

The tinkle of the brook flowing under the bridge could be easily heard in the frosty silence.

Max stopped short and pointed.

"What the heck is *that*?"

"It looks like a jack o' lantern," said Katya.

Near the middle of the bridge was an enormous pumpkin with a grinning face carved into it. An uncanny light—perhaps it was a candle—emanated from the eyes and mouth and cast an eerie glow that caught the sparkles and crystals of the snow on the railing and deck in its luminosity.

"It's an omen," said Katya. Katya's Ukrainian family were highly superstitious people.

"It's weird," said Robert.

"Who would light a jack o'lantern in the middle of winter in the middle of nowhere?" said Max.

"Somebody who wanted to scare somebody," said Robert.

Katya and Margot huddled together and Charmaine pulled her coat tighter around her shoulders.

"I don't see footprints—none!" said Perry. "Which is impossible since somebody had to have been here."

"This is really creepy," said Margot.

Charmaine agreed. "So now what?"

"We wait," said Robert.

"For what?" The girls looked at him.

To their surprise, Robert suddenly cupped his hands and shouted: "Come out and show yourself. We came here just for *you!*"

That sent a wave of shivers through all of them. Not the yelling, but that Robert was dead on the money—they *did* come in the anticipation of seeing a ghost or apparition; they *expected* it, they *wanted* it!

All around them, as if in answer, the group began to see faces in the snowbanks, or leering down from snow-laden boughs. The whole mood of the place changed.

The little group of friends huddled together now as they stood only a few yards from the center of the span.

Something—probably a bird—screeched in the nearby woods.

Katya was clinging to Margot for dear life.

Then they saw it. It was coming toward them from the far end of the bridge.

    "Be careful what you wish for..." Perry could be heard to mutter.

All that could be seen was a brilliant star of light, about chest height, hovering in thin air, gold or silvery—it was hard to tell it was so intense.

As it drew nearer it appeared to stream from a lantern, and that lantern was carried by a girl of about sixteen, with a pearlescent gown that touched the ground with what seemed to be a magical light of its own.

The thin arm raised the lantern aloft so the curve of her face and the glitter of her eyes were revealed.

"That's her. That's Sylvia Martin. Or it's the spitting image of her," Charmaine said. Her voice trembled.

"What do you want from us?" Again, Robert spoke out, and if he was frightened, he sure didn't show it.

"She's pointing down, to the railing—no! To the water!" Max said.

"Something to do with the water?" Robert half-shouted. He seemed to be unsure what the ghost would do next.

In the time it took for their pounding hearts to hammer out another beat, the light withdrew into the lantern, and the apparition was snuffed out like a candle.

The entire bunch of them stood on a dark bridge where only the sound of running water could be again heard.

CHAPTER FOURTEEN   THE CRASH

"I'm telling you, it's something about the creek, the water," said Robert.

"She died in that creek, remember?" Charmaine said.

"Oh my gawd," said Katya. "How come I don't know this?"

"You had already left for Connecticut when it happened," said Rita.

"This is the ghostly hitchhiker, isn't it?" said Henry, who was over his cold, and upset that he missed all the excitement at Lantern Bridge.

"She wants us to pay attention to the water, like there's something there we need to know," Charmaine said.

"Maybe it's a warning," said Margot.

"Well, the odds of another car crashing through the railing on that particular bridge is vanishingly small," said Perry.

Robert agreed.

"What's everyone doing for New Year's?" asked Margot.

"I'm watching movies at my house if anyone wants to come," said Robert. "My parents will be out at a party so we have the whole place to ourselves."

"I might come," said Max.

"Katya and I might come too, if that's okay. It's not a 'boys-only' event, right?" Margot inquired.

"Oh no, just us Malt Shop people eating five topping pizza and guzzling root beer," laughed Robert. "I got the full DVD set of *Star Trek* for Christmas. We are going to watch the whole series."

"The movies or the TV series?" said Henry.

"The movies. We already have the Gene Roddenberry series on DVD, and the *Next Generation* as well."

"Wow, Robert! I didn't know you were a Trekkie!" said Henry.

"It's my Dad, really, who turned me on to the Star Trek thing. He grew up with it," said Robert.

"Maybe I will come then; will you come too, Perry?" said Henry beseechingly.

"Sure. Count me in. Thanks for hosting us, Robert. And thanks for covering the cost of our little adventure the other night."

"You are most welcome, Perry. We do have the most unusual adventures when you are around," Robert said.

"Hey! It's not *me*! It's like I am the designated target of the Fates when they get bored and want to mess with Humans."

So it was all settled: Robert's house, 9 p.m. December 31st. It would be a peaceful night for everyone.

Almost everyone.

***

The ice and snow had now been mainly cleared off the back roads by the County, but temperatures remained below freezing, sometimes well below freezing.

This freeze-thaw cycle made driving hazardous, and state and local police were out trying to stop drunk drivers, who usually turned out to be partygoers too cheap to take a cab.

But it was not alcohol that played a part of the crash that happened some time after midnight on New Year's Eve.

The crash happened at Lantern Bridge, six miles outside of town, and the very place that a young lady died eighteen months before when her drunken boyfriend lost control of the car and it plunged twenty feet or so into the cold water of Brandywine Creek, a tributary of the Seneca River, that flows to Lake Cayuga.

Officer (actually Sergeant)Van Cleef was the first on the scene.

He radioed for an ambulance and a tow truck.

He gingerly clambered over the railing on the west shore to get down to the creek itself. He well knew as a policeman and highway patrolman--seconds count in life-or-death situations that law enforcement officers often find themselves in.

"Anybody hear me? Are you OK?" He was hollering at the wrecked vehicle, nose down in the gravel, water up to the windows flowing cold and fast.

"Please! Help!" A girl's voice called out.

Officer Van Cleef had no pole, no lifejackets or boots for wading into the freezing creek. He climbed back to his car and retrieved a length of rope from the trunk, and then leaped over the railing and down the bank again.

The bowline is the best knot for rescue: it won't slip and it gives enough rope for a person to slip it over their head and under their armpits.

He tossed the rope so that it would hook on the passenger side mirror.

"Get the rope! Slip it over your shoulders and let me pull you out the window!"

This was going to be dicey, he knew. One mistake and a life might be lost. He wished right now that he had some backup, some other bodies to haul on the rope, or wade out to the car.

But law enforcement in this small town in upstate New York was usually just one person: him!

Sure, he had a deputy-- who just happened to have the night off and who had gone to Rochester to visit his parents.

The girl, amazingly, was halfway out of the car and Officer Van Cleef anchored the rope on a steel girder and pulled with all he had.

With a mighty tug she slipped through the window, and screamed when the icy water soaked her to the skin.

But within a minute or two, she was onshore—shivering but safe.

"Get in the cruiser. Who was driving?"

"My boyfriend Jerry. Do you think he's...".

"No! Now get in my car, start the engine and put the heat on full. An ambulance should be on the way."

Van Cleef took the rope and slung the bight over his own shoulders and waded out into the creek.

He could see the driver was unconscious; he didn't smell alcohol so he decided the impact had knocked him out.

The seat belt wouldn't release. Half-in and half-out of the wrecked Chevy, he dug out a service knife and cut Jerry free. There was only one rope so the officer slung it over the victim's head and under the one arm he could reach, and started lugging—inch by inch— on the unconscious boy.

At that moment—a miracle!

"Jake! Jake!" A couple of guys were over the railing and tossing another rope to the cop who was having trouble remaining stable in the swift current.

Somehow—between the three of them—they hauled the kid out of the water and up to the ambulance, where an EMT laid him on a cot and hooked him up to oxygen and an IV drip.

The girl asked permission--and it was granted, so she could ride to the hospital with him.

"You sure know how to pick 'em, Jake!" joked the ambulance driver, having a smoke behind the squad car.

"They don't pay me extra to go jumping off bridges into icy creeks, Paul," said Sargent Jacob Van Cleef of the Brackendale Police Department. "Comes with the job!"

"You know these kids? Probably too much partying!"

"No, I didn't smell liquor or weed on them. I think they took the rise before the bridge too fast and the black ice did the rest," said Officer Van Cleef.

"They're damn lucky, if you ask me. Remember that girl who drowned two summers ago? Same damn situation; went over the edge in a car."

"I remember, Paul. She was just a middle-school student with an older guy who didn't have the sense to drive sober. This bridge is getting a history.

"You take them to Brackendale General, I'm going to wait for the wrecker. I called him two hours ago, but then—it's New Year's Eve. He must be pretty busy."

Chapter Fifteen   The Gold Watch

The car had been hauled out and towed back to town by the time Perry and the gang got the news.

"How did *you* find out?" Charmaine asked Margot.

"I know her. She's Chinese too. My parents go to church with *her* parents. Word gets around in the Asian community; we have our own grapevine, you know!"

"Who was the guy? Had he been drinking? Or toking?"

"No. He's Chinese as well. Chinese kids don't do drugs as a rule. I think he was just showing off his new Toyota and lost control on the bridge."

Charmaine nodded.

Rita came into the diner and slid in beside her.

"Hey? Have you heard about the crash at Lantern Bridge?"

Charmaine said: "Margot is way ahead of you. Nobody badly hurt but a couple of kids got the scare of their life, I'm guessing."

"How about we go out to the bridge? Check around. See if the Toyota left anything behind. I doubt the tow truck driver would search carefully. What if this girl's purse or wallet is still at the bottom of the creek?"

Margot was right.

"Yeah, that's a good idea. We should check. But is it safe?" said Rita.

"I'm going to phone Officer Van Cleef and get his take on it," said Charmaine.

"Margot, you contact this girl and see if she is missing something from the wreck, just in case we find something out there."

"Okay, sure. I'll ask my Mom. Do we need boots? I will bring them. Somebody call Robert. It's time for The Malt Shop gang to go to work!"

***

"Let's start with a hypothesis," said Perry. "The ghosts both haunt this particular bridge. I understand why the poor girl in her spirit body is tethered by her sudden death to that place. Most ghost-hunters agree that this is common."

"That *what* is common," said Robert.

"That a ghost hangs around the place they died because there is some unfinished business. Only they can't find closure because they are not in physical form any longer so they can't, like, bury their bones or find a lost will or document."

"Okay, that might explain the girl, but what about the soldier in blue? He's the original reason for naming the bridge 'Lantern Bridge'!" said Robert.

"This I don't know," said Perry.

"Margot proposes we make a trip out there, as soon as possible, to, like, look for stuff," Charmaine said.

"I can arrange it," said Robert. "When?"

"Tomorrow," said Charmaine.

"I'll get Henry on board," Perry said, putting on his jacket.

"Too bad Katya had to go back. She will miss the next exciting installment of 'The Ghost of Lantern Bridge'. We should make a video and post it on YouTube!"

"Meet at my place, like before," said Robert as he left the diner.

"This is going to be wicked!" said Charmaine dropping her voice to a whisper, since everyone had already left and there was no one left to say it to.

***

"Officer Van Cleef was quite helpful and doesn't see a problem if we go out there, but he did caution us to take some ropes if we are wading into the creek.

The weatherman said there will be no snow or rain for the next few days, and water levels in ponds, creeks and dams will be dropping. We might just luck out!" Charmaine said.

"Here comes the taxi," said Robert. "Same guy. I think he's starting to like us!"

The minivan pulled into the rest area about 50 yards from the bridge, and the gang piled out with packs and a couple of polypropylene ropes about fifty feet long.

Max, Robert, Henry and Perry led the troop to the railing where they could slither down the bank close to where the wrecked car had lain.

"Henry! You were good at knots and lashing stuff when we did that paramilitary training two summers ago. How about you lasso a log on the far side so we

have a rope right across to hold on to." Robert
pointed to a stump that looked suitable.

Henry did it with expert aim, and using a slip knot,
tightened the rope and anchored it on a beam under
the bridge.

"Who's first?" said Robert.

"Me—me!" said Margot, with her knee-high rubber
boots already in the water.

"I think the water's dropped a couple of feet from
when we were last here," said Max.

"All the better. Henry, did you bring the halogen
flashlights you said you had at home?"

"Yup, I did Robert. I got two that I've fully charged."

"Okay, ready to rock?" said Robert.

By tying each member to the main rope that spanned
the stream, each one of them was able to participate.

The weather was clear and the sun was high in the
sky, and it almost felt like an early Spring was coming.

"Hey-yaa! I've found something!" Margot pulled
Rita's hand and the others crowded around.

In the bottom of a pool sheltered by a ring of rocks, something glinted in the sun. Something gold.

"Fish it out!" said Max. "Here. Let me."

Max pushed up his right sleeve and reached down into the crystal clear pool. It was only a matter of inches to the gravel and smooth stones at the bottom. Tangled around a stone was a gold chain.

"What's on the other end?" Everybody wanted to know.

"Can't tell yet. Wait." Max swept some sand and lifted one of the granite stones from the bottom.

"It's an old watch! You know, like your granddad used to have," said Max.

He held it to the sun and Perry took off his glove and dried the glittery object, tipping it slightly to drain it from under the closed cover.

"This must be worth something," said Robert.

"We should show Mr. Caygeon—he might know," said Henry. "Hey! There's initials carved into the lid: HYS."

"*Henry Gerrit Schuyler*," said Max with a smile.

"No, Max. That would be H*GS*," said Henry.

"Put it into your pack, Henry. Let's keep looking. Maybe there's other stuff in this creek," said Robert.

"Over here!" shouted Margot.

"Geez, eagle-eyes there finds everything!" said Rita. "What is it, Margot?"

"Looks like a locket. Has a silver chain, really thin one, but it's still intact. Must belong to a girl."

"Wonder where it came from? Washed down from upstream?" Max was studying the delicate item.

"Okay—I am going to say it," said Charmaine. "What if this belongs to...the ghost girl...to Sylvia Martin?"

"How do we find out?" said Margot.

"We will have to contact her family. They will be able to recognize it as something that belonged to their daughter, right?"

"Yeah, that makes sense," said Margot. "Here. Put it in my pouch. Careful! Don't drop it. I don't want to go poking through this stream any more than I have to. Is anyone else getting cold?"

Everyone was.

"Shall we continue?" said Henry.

"I think we have enough treasure for one day, Capt. Jack Sparrow!" said Robert, comparing Henry to the mythical pirate of the Caribbean.

Robert waved the taxi toward the bridge and they all piled in, relieved to be sitting down in a warm place, and ready to go home.

"Tomorrow. At Henry's place. Bring the watch and the locket. Snacks are on Henry!" Charmaine seemed pleased with what they had found.

***

"This watch needs an expert. What about Old Jenkins at the jewelry store?" Henry was speaking.

"Sure, we could try asking him," said Rita.

"The other thing I was thinking was that Bob Caygeon might know something about it. I mean it looks *really* old, like over a hundred years old."

"Older than Miss Floon?" chirped Robert.

"That was mean," said Charmaine. "Take it back!"

"Okay, sorry to insult the old dear," said Robert.

"Let's give custody—if we can call it that—of the silver locket and chain to Margot. For now. And we'll give Henry custody of the gold watch and gold chain. Once we find out more, we can make a decision."

Perry was convincing, perhaps because he was so rational, so sensible. That's what his teachers said, and that's what his buddies thought as well.

***

Old Mr. Jenkins took the jeweler's loupe—a little magnifying glass—from his left eye.

"Well, it's real gold, I can tell you that. As for the date, it must be early 1800s or so. The detailing in the gold case is something they haven't done for many many years. Are you lookin' to sell it?"

"No," said Henry. "I just want to know more about it."

"Well, where did you get it? Garage sale?"

"No sir. I found it. Ah, while out walking in the woods."

"Well, if you change your mind, I'll give you a decent dollar for it."

Henry thanked the old jeweler, got on his bike and headed down to the Museum of American History to see the curator Bob Caygeon.

"Must be late 18th Century or early 19th Century Henry. Where did you pick this up?"

"Everybody asks me that. I'm not sure what to say. I found it with my friends, Mr. Caygeon."

"*Found it*? Where?"

"In the creek out by Lantern Bridge."

"That where the car went over at New Year's?"

"Yes sir. Do you think *they* lost it?"

"Based on what you told me about where it was found—I doubt it."

Mr. Caygeon took a thin knife and carefully pried open the cover. Water had got in, but this watch had not been opened for a very long time.

"Look, Henry. There's a compartment in the lid. Let me see if I can...open it..."

He very slowly wedged his blade under the thin plate of gold nestled in the inside cover of the watch.

"Well I'll be damned!" The words just jumped out of his mouth. "Look what we have here!"

Henry leaned in and over the table. A small scrap of paper was inside. Mr. Caygeon put on his white gloves and took a pair of tweezers from his drawer.

Unfolding the paper, he said: "Looks like a map, Henry. Some kind of map. Must give directions for something. It was carefully hidden in the lid of this watch for a reason."

"And what about the engraved initials on the outside, Mr. Caygeon. The *HYS*?"

"That is part of the mystery here, Henry. What we have here is a gen-yoo-wine mystery!"

"A map? Really? That is awesome," said Max.

"Did he open it up, Henry?" said Perry.

"Yes, but neither of us could make any sense of it. On the north part of the map was a lake. And on the south part was a bunch of doodles that looked like trees and stones, maybe they are landmarks."

"So there's a treasure within the treasure," said Perry.

"So what do you think it could be?" said Henry.

"Whoever owned this watch left a map for someone to find, maybe he was dying or going to be killed, and he wanted the treasure to be found."

"That makes sense. Wait a minute…! Is this somehow connected to the phantom soldier at Lantern Bridge? Was this *his* watch? His secret?"

"I think you are on to something here, Henry. The ghost is waving the lamp and often seen peering down, where the creek is. Does he want people to find something he lost there?"

"It's the only thing that makes sense, Perry. Why else would he haunt that particular bridge?"

"Well, we are going to *listen*, Henry. This is a mystery that has come to us to solve, and by golly! We're gonna do it!"

***

"Let's approach this from another angle, Henry. We have no way of knowing what the map leads to— if anything. It might be the equivalent of a property deed, a land claim.

But if Mr. Caygeon is willing, we might try and do another DNA test using the watch. What do you think?"

"I think that after 200 years in the water that there will be zero DNA to work with. Think about it, Perry."

"Yeah, I know you are right, but what if the innermost compartment—the one with the map, just may, *may* have a miniscule trace of the owner's DNA. Can we afford to not explore this possibility, Henry?"

"What will that tell us? They won't find a match because there's no one to match it to. It's not like we have someone who claims to be the relative of the

owner of this artifact. Maybe Old Jenkins." Henry
was being sarcastic.

"Anyway, let's ask Mr. Caygeon if he can get his
New York contacts to work their magic one more
time."

"That gives us *two* directions to go in: the genetics,
and the map. But I have another idea that is so crazy
I wonder if I am losing my mind." Perry looked at his
hands and then the floor and then at Henry.

"Everything you and I do is crazy, Perry."

"Okay so listen, Henry. I keep thinking about the
initials HYS on the cover. And I keep thinking about
Hon Yost and whether Benjamin Arnold gave him
some kind of reward for the sacrifice he made. You
know what I'm saying?"

"HYS. Hon Yost Schuyler. Eh Perry? Could this
watch be a gift from the general to Hon Yost Schuyler
for service to his country? Gold watch? Makes sense.
They used to give employees who worked their
whole life for a corporation a gold watch upon
retirement.

But how on earth did it end up in a creek between
Brackendale and Lake Cayuga? Fort Stanwix is over a
hundred miles in the other direction, where the city

of Rome is now. Unless....unless he was carrying it and he lost it, or someone ended his life and....no, no. Too many 'ifs'."

"No, Henry, keep brainstorming the possibilities. Whatever the truth turns out to be, it's going to be strange and unbelievable.

What I think we need to do is to go back to the historical record and find out what actually happened to the man, after Arnold came to the fort and found that his clever ruse using Hon Yost had actually saved the fort and avoided further conflict with both British and Mohawk fighters.

Is this making sense to you?"

"It's brilliant, Perry. It gives us a three-prong strategy to solving the mystery of the watch.

To the library!"

***

"Look here, Henry. This is an account of St. Leger's attempt to close off the Mohawk Valley and hook up with Burgoyne. Look what his journal says:

It has occurred to me that all my effort to suppress these rebels may be in vain. Upon viewing this pitiful wooden stockade they hide behind, I see that their

*banner hung high on the rampart reveals their deeper
sentiment. It is a flag, no doubt, with the same three
colors but arranged strangely: stars in one corner,
stripes on the face of the thing. Stars and stripes! I will
tear it down personally and trample it underfoot.*

"There was an *American flag*, Henry! And they flew
it on Ft. Stanwix! Can we find alternate sources that
can prove this? Find out if there were any reports or
news items that could possibly verify this."

"When I type in keywords 'Stars and stripes' or
'American flag' I get three hits on newspapers of the
time. First is the *Boston Gazette* the most important
media outlet of the day, and I get *Pennsylvania
evening Post* and *Pennsylvania Journal.*

Let me see if I can correlate the flag comments
with the war in New York.

Perry! Look! There it is in black and white! I
cannot believe it! Look, look!"

There was a small article in the *Pennsylvania Evening
Journal* that reported that the British had been
repulsed at both Fort Stanwix and Saratoga. That
General Benedict Arnold had made direct reference
to the 'flag replete with our stars and strypes' that
flew so proudly over the ramparts at Ft. Stanwix

when he 'arrived—not in haste--but in victorious
fashion'. Arnold saw the flag, Perry!"

"So where is that flag now?"

"The Boston paper says that the Second
Continental Congress specified that stars and stripes
make up the new flag and is was passed as a law in
the colonies. How interesting!

Here's another piece from the *Pennsylvania Journal*,
that everyone in Philadelphia must have been reading,
to say that Capt. Abraham Swartout who was part of
the American defense at Ft. Stanwix, was paid cash
for the use of his blue coat in the making of that flag.
There's even a receipt that was given to him.

The red came from flannel sleepwear and the white
from a soldier's shirt. Some soldier at Ft. Stanwix
gave the shirt off his back—literally, to make the very
first American flag."

"Where is that flag, Henry? It was at Fort Stanwix
in August of 1777. It would be a national treasure,
and hopefully it ended up with Arnold's men and got
locked away—like Gen. Schuyler's sword.

Let's see what we can find out about that.

Back to the museum. I 've got a feeling Mr. Bob Caygeon knows more that he lets on."

"I know one thing, boys, there has been a lot of debate about America's first flag. Some continue to believe that Betsy Ross—a Philadelphia upholsterer made the first flag, although the evidence suggests she only modified it later, and she never even met George Washington.

Then there was Francis Hopkinson who claimed to have designed it. But many scholars say it was a simple modification of the Grand Union Flag. The real story we may never know."

"Well, Henry and I have a theory, sir. Like to hear it?"

"Of course, Perry. You have been doing some digging in the Library, haven't you?"

Perry told the curator what they had found out, and read in news accounts.

"That's interesting," said Mr. Caygeon. "An eyewitness to the surrender of Burgoyne at Saratoga described seeing a flag with thirteen stars in a circle in the upper left corner, and thirteen stripes of red and white alternately on the field or fly. The witness said it represented the Thirteen Colonies now united in a common cause.

That would put your flag at Fort Stanwix very near to the place of victory that Arnold and Gates stood only a month later! So there is good reason to believe this is the original, the very first flag of the United States of America."

Perry stood up and paced back and forth, the way George Washington would do when faced with a decision.

"I'm prepared, gentlemen," he said speaking only to the curator and Henry, of course, "...to conclude that this flag was made in haste at Fort Stanwix, and carried secretly—possibly by Hon Yost—to Saratoga and openly presented for the first time by Benedict Arnold himself.

This would have been the glorious moment to show the British that America was *real*, that it was not a proposition on a piece of paper, but a country of living breathing men and women 'dedicated to the proposition that all men are created equal'."

"Why, Perry, I think you've hit on it! I think you have really unraveled the mystery of the first flag and where it first appeared in American history!"

Bob Caygeon was so excited that he pulled open a drawer at his desk and took out a small bottle of what looked like whisky, and filled a small glass—draining it like a man dying of thirst.

He didn't offer the boys any--who would not have accepted anyway.

Mr. Caygeon suddenly seemed shy, and placed the bottle and the glass in its convenient hiding place, and turned to the boys and said:

   "So where is this flag *now* I wonder. I would give all I have to have it here—in our museum!"

Perry looked at Henry, and said: "We want to see that map again. The one in the watch. I have the strangest feeling there may be a clue to solving two mysteries on our hands: who is the ghost of Lantern Bridge? And where is America's lost flag?"

"The thing that bugs me, Henry, is where did Hon Yost get such an expensive gold watch? Did he steal it and have his own name carved into the cover? I doubt it."

"I doubt it too, Perry. What if General Arnold went back to Fort Dayton, to later rendezvous with Gen. Gates at that farm at Saratoga? And what if he decided to allow his faithful recruit Hon Yost Schuyler to accompany him as a matter of honor?"

"Spell it out, Henry! Where is this going?"

"That would explain how the flag ended up at Saratoga—Hon Yost would have been the flag-bearer. Gen. Arnold had a watch engraved for him as a token of his gratitude for extraordinary service.

Without the collapse of the British thrust at Ft. Stanwix, there would not have been an American victory at Saratoga. Arnold knew that. Arnold knew he owed a great debt to this brave young man. And being the great man he was, Benedict Arnold gave him a golden gift to last a lifetime!"

"You must be right, Henry. It's logical. It's consistent with the facts," said Perry.

"So, what about the flag?"

Henry pulled up a chair and put his feet on Perry's bed.

"Well, that brings us to the map. Why would Hon Yost make a secret map and hide it in the only thing he owned that was precious or valuable?"

"That means the map must be equally valuable," said Perry. "Whatever information that map contains may have been worth dying for. I am more convinced that ever that our ghost in uniform is none other than Hon Yost Schuyler.

And the reason he won't leave, the reason he haunts Lantern Bridge is that he wanted us to find his watch—and find the map!"

"This is the answer, Perry. We have the answer."

"But there is one thing left to do, now that we believe we know the secret. We have to use the map and find the treasure—whatever it may be—that Hon Yost hid before he died."

***

"This is a wild goose chase, boys," said Mr. Caygeon. "Why do you think this map leads to any kind of treasure?"

"Because it is where it *is*. Don't you see? The owner, whoever it was, wanted whoever found his watch to find the map and the treasure."

Perry and Henry were in the back room of the museum.

"Here. We brought you a Grande Cappucino from the Starbuck's 'cause we know that's your fav," said Perry.

"Thank you very much, Perry. Some days I just need a shot of caffeine."

And some days you need a shot of something you hide in your lower right drawer, Perry was thinking with a smile.

Mr. Caygeon opened the watch and extracted the map carefully and lay it on the table. He began to scan it with a magnifying glass.

Perry and Henry were also looking closely, making a few notes. What did it all mean? What did the weird symbols say?

"Let's assume that this map—although not to scale—has 'North' at the top, and 'South' at the bottom. What we see is a body of water, and a

village—that's what the little square houses stand for.
The trees are forested areas."

"What about this one? I can't read the writing,"
said Perry. "He used some soluble kind of ink that
has faded over time."

"It looks like a fence," said Henry. "In a circle. With
a house or building in the middle. It's Fort Stanwix!
See! There's one cannon in the courtyard, and then a
ditch kind of thing with several cannon pointed at the
fort. It's a bird's eye view of the fort!"

"Okay," said Mr. Caygeon. "I can buy that. It is
located in the northeast of the map, where it would
appear on any normal map. Going southwest from
there, we cross a river and enter a forest, pass a small
village…wait!"

"The village has teepees; that must mean it is an
Indian village, not a white settlement," said Henry.

"He was crossing Indian land. Going where?" said
Perry.

"What is the farthest point southwest on this map,
Mr. Caygeon? What does it show?"

"Fields. Nothing. Just open land. Wait! There's a
symbol like an upside-down 'U'. And what looks like

a really tiny American flag inside. What does that mean?"

Perry and Henry looked at each other and shrugged.

"Let me see," said Perry, unconsciously giving Mr. Caygeon a little nudge to make room for himself.

"Maybe that was the journey's end. He wanted to mark it somehow," said Perry.

"Maybe he died there, Perry," said Henry.

"Maybe he had a relative—or even a girlfriend there," said Mr. Caygeon, with a wink.

"So how did his gold watch end up in a creek outside of our little town? said Perry.

"I can think of only two ways, Perry," said Henry.

"One way is that it fell into a body of water, that is—he lost it, and it was carried down the Seneca River to our Brandywine Creek by spring floods."

"Over two hundred years?" said Perry. "Give me another hypothesis."

"The only other way that comes to mind is that someone found him dead, and picked his pocket, or someone found the watch laying in the dirt after he lost it, and took it with them to trade or sell later."

"That makes more sense to me," said the curator, swallowing the last of the coffee and tossing the cup into the wastebasket.

"Hey, give me that cup, I will recycle it," said Henry.

"So what we are saying here is that Hon Yost lost his gold watch, but not before scribbling a crude map showing the landscape where he was situated and hiding it in the lid."

"That's right, Perry, and the watch was dropped into the creek, probably when there was no bridge and you had to wade across, and was lost. Lost until a freak car accident revealed its resting place. And came into your hands, Mr. Perry Normal," said Mr. Caygeon.

"Now that would make an incredible story, wouldn't it? Somebody should write a book!" he said.

"So we have come full circle—we found the watch and we found the map, but we still don't know where any of these places marked on it are, or why they were put there." Perry was pacing again.

"I know someone who may be able to help us," said Perry at length.

"Who?" said Henry and Mr. Caygeon in the same breath.

"Wolf Skin. Tekanantokin. Remember when we asked him where the traditional Oneida land was, and he said: 'You're standing on it'?"

"Yeah, I remember," Henry said.

"Let's send him an e-mail request. If he is willing to come take us to where this map leads, we just might find what the owner of this watch wanted to be found!"

***

"Hey, my paleface brothers!" The old Ford pickup pulled up outside the Malt Shop, and Wolf Skin stepped out and shook their hands.

"Sure is good to see you, Wolf Skin," said Henry.

"Good to see you guys too. What is going on down here in Brackendale?"

"Henry and I have a problem, and we think the only one who can help us with it is you." Perry looked directly at Wolf Skin.

"I get it. You want me to teach you how to hunt wearing nothing but wolfskins, eh? Am I right?"

All three were convulsed with laughter and merriment for a time.

The food came and they tucked in to a diner meal hungrily.

"We didn't bring you all the way down here from your home for nothing," Perry began.

"I made a scanned copy of a map that we found in a mysterious way. Thing is, I think the map shows Oneida land and some kind of secret related to it. It came from a white soldier who fought for the American side at Ft. Stanwix, and who—I believe—left behind some kind of...artifact or object, that Henry and I--and other people too—would like to find. It may have great historical significance for New York, for the whole country."

"Wow! That's heavy, man!" Wolf Skin had eyes like a wolf—yellowish-brown and full of intelligence.

"Show me the map," he said, wiping his mouth and fingers with a napkin, and moving his plate to make room for the black-and-white photocopy of the map.

" Looks to me like someone buried something, made a cache, not that far from this village. These are teepees, by the way. My people had more permanent dwellings made of logs and material from the forest. 'Teepee' is a Sioux invention. They are Plains Indians and traveled on horseback. They needed these light skin tents to shelter on cold Dakota nights.

As I was saying, this symbol like a dome with a flag is likely to be where it—whatever it is—is stashed.

We can take a run out there in my truck. I know the Oneida who live in that village, been there for generations. I live there too. And of course, it's Indian land."

"You've got a deal, Wolf Skin!"

Perry and Henry were shifting and wriggling in the booth like two fish in a net.

"I'm gonna stay with my friend in town. I will meet you here for breakfast at 7:30—can you get up that early on a weekend?"

"We shall be here," said Perry.

"Good! Bring some lunch! It's gonna be a long day."

Wolf Skin stepped on the running board on the driver's side and swung into the seat, firing up the motor as if in one movement.

"I want a truck so I can do that," said Henry.

Perry slung his right arm over Henry's shoulders, and off they went full of hope that tomorrow might bring the answer to everything!

CHAPTER EIGHTEEN   THE TREASURE

It was overcast as the pickup headed east on Hwy.20 then north to the I-90, then east toward Syracuse and Lake Oneida.

"My people occupy some of the good farmland south of the Lake. The Oneida reservation is bigger than that, of course, but we are going to try to zero in on exactly where that map wants to take us."

They stopped for gas. Perry and Henry both handed Wolf Skin some cash, which he appreciated. Wolf Skin came out with a coffee. They were making good time, he said.

Near Canastota he turned north on a side road, which then led to a narrow lane, full of puddles and mud.

"Pardon the washboard, fellas."

Perry took that to mean the rough road and potholes, which it did.

At length, Wolf Skin pulled into a yard where a small frame house and a couple of trailers were situated.

"Come on in and meet my wife and kids," he said.

"Hello. Welcome to our village," said a small attractive woman who seemed awfully young, until their two kids came running out of the bedroom to greet them.

"Who are they, Daddy?" said the girl who was about eight or nine. Her brother was about five. They had bare feet and longish hair, and were constantly chasing each other with happy cries.

"This is Perry. This is Henry. They are helping me today out in the south fields."

Perry knew that he did not want them to tag along on this adventure—they would just get in the way. This was a serious matter, not for children.

Mrs. Wolf Skin seemed to understand and shushed the children back into the back of the house.

"Ready?"

"We're ready," said Perry.

Wolf Skin slipped into a wood frame packboard which he fitted with a rope, a short shovel, and a rifle. They set out in a southwest direction. They were following the map, a map made over two hundred years ago by a man with an unknown purpose, crossing Oneida land.

"There's the forest, I think. Looks like it. What do you think, Perry?"

"Distances are hard to gage on this map. But you are right, we need to find landmarks that appear to match the map."

Henry said: "My boots hurt. Can we stop for a second so I can loosen the laces and pull my socks up?"

A slight wind coming from the north off Lake Oneida ruffled their hair, and carried the scent of coming Spring. Birds flocked overhead to find nests along its shore.

They tramped on in the same direction.

"Don't you need a compass to tell which direction you are going?" asked Henry.

"I'm an Indian," said Wolf Skin, smiling. "I know by instinct."

They came at length to a clearing. It was in a circle of round granite stones, each weighing probably 150 pounds. Circles mean something, Perry knew.

So did Wolf Skin.

"Let's stop here and get a feel for where we are. There should be something on the ground that is represented by this upside-down 'U' shape with the flag-thing under it. It signifies something was left here, I'm guessing. The 'U' is a symbol for a cache—a place where you leave food, or a tool."

Perry sat on a boulder. "This is an erratic. Carried here by glacial ice. It's a rock that does not match the local bedrock."

Henry laughed and explained to Wolf Skin that they were junior scientists and looked at the world as a giant scientific playground; that included geology.

Henry was stepping out of the circle to get a better look at the landscape when suddenly he broke through the rotten planks covered in leaves and moss, and plunged about ten feet into a hole. Or what looked like a hole.

The two rushed over and Wolf Skin snaked the rope down to the floor of what looked like a cave.

"I'm okay," said Henry, " just shaken up. I didn't see the boards."

"What *is* this place?" said Perry.

"I never come down this way on the band property, so I have no idea. It's like a room in a cave." Wolf Skin shone a flashlight into the shadows.

"Could this be the upside down 'U'? asked Perry.

"Then where is the thing represented by a flag?" said Wolf Skin.

"Right here," said Henry, "...exactly...right...here."

He was kneeling by a wooden box with a metal lock having green powder where it was eaten away.

"Brass!" said Henry and Perry at once.

"Open it, Henry."

"You got a knife, Wolf Skin?"

He slid the narrow blade from a sheath he wore on a leather thong around his neck.

"Indian-style," he said with a grin.

Henry worked the blade under the rotten brass clasp and it yielded.

What lay inside caused all three of them to gasp!

It was a piece of cloth, carefully folded three times on itself, and a piece of paper quite yellowed with age beneath.

The boys realized at once what the cloth was.

"This is what we came for, Wolf Skin. This is the real treasure we have been seeking."

Perry softly unfolded the flag with the indigo-blue corner and its circle of crudely but lovingly sewn white stars—thirteen in all.

The red and white stripes smelled of mold and damp, but their colors remained bold and vivid.

"This is Hon Yost's legacy to his country," said Perry solemnly. "He would be so pleased that it will see the sunlight once more, in an America he helped create."

Wolf Skin took his Yankees cap off and touched his chest.

Henry almost wanted to cry, so he sneezed from the dust instead.

"We couldn't have done it without you, Tekanatokin—he of the Wolf Skin! We are going to make sure that your name goes into the history books and your kids will know that Indian people are an equal part of that history. I swear to you, I will help it happen!"

Wolf Skin embraced Perry and shook his hand.

"This is a glad day for the Oneida people. What does the parchment say?"

"We forgot about the letter, Perry, in all the excitement. What *does* it say?"

Wolf Skin shone the light full on the brown page.

To whomever reads this. I, Hon Yost Schuyler, have lain down my body but my spirit will not rest until this noble banner that was given into my keeping by General Benedict Arnold in the Year 1777 and ten months be restored to its rightful place in the hands of the American People.

It was by the General's gracious act and deed that I came to possess it. It was he who spake the secret that my own father dare not—I am the son, illegitimate I was told, of General Philip Schuyler of the Continental Army of New York.

I am content to know, and to have touched the flag to which all soldiers who are patriots pledged their life and liberty. In God We Trust.

"Look! His initials: HYS." Henry traced them with his fingertips.

"Henry Yost Schuyler is your blood relative, Henry. He is your family. So this flag now belongs to you!"

Perry held his friend as tears welled up in their eyes.

"It belongs to all of us," Henry said.

***

"Can we see it? Can we touch it, like just for a moment?" Charmaine and the gang were waiting for Perry and Henry once they got the e-mail.

They were at Henry's house, and his parents and friends were all there to see this marvelous treasure for themselves.

"What are you going to do with it?" asked Max. "Sell it? You could make a mint on E-Bay!"

"Shut up, Max," said Robert. "This is a priceless relic, like the Mask of Tutankhamun! Nobody's going to sell *that*!"

"Well I think my parents will agree that it should be given to the Museum of American History in our lovely hometown of Brackendale."

"Wait till Bob Caygeon sees this," said Rita.

"He is so gonna freak!" said Charmaine.

"Should I mention the letter now, Dad?" asked Henry.

"Go ahead, Henry. It fits with the whole story, actually."

"There was a handwritten…note…I guess you could call it, in the box with the flag."

Henry read it aloud. The expression on everyone's face would have made a great Facebook post, Margot was thinking.

"Are you kidding me?" Charmaine always calls it like she sees it. "How many Schuylers are going to be heroes in New York history?"

"Henry will!" said Max and Margot together, patting Henry on the shoulder affectionately.

***

"This is truly a gift of a lifetime to our museum, Henry."

Flashes from cameras made Mr. Caygeon look pale and old but he had a million-dollar smile on his face.

TV reporters were fiddling with videocams and mikes, newspapers from as far away as New York City and Philadelphia had people there.

The mayor wanted to call it a 'media circus' but then it put his little town in the spotlight in a very good way. So he strutted up and down the sidewalk, giving interviews—as if he personally had sponsored the recovery of this national treasure.

So, Hon Yost's flag found a worthy home at last. Strange to say, the ghost of Lantern Bridge was not seen again, at least not by anyone alive today in Brackendale.

***

There were two things left for Perry and Henry to do.

They were putting together a podcast to maybe be aired on National Public Radio that would help balance the opinion of history about Benedict Arnold. It was clear that most of Arnold's military career was to help America win its independence.

But first they had to pay a visit to the librarian, Miss Floon.

"We want to share with you all our research that has gone into our audio project," said Perry.

"We want you to use it in your book about your distant relative and your complex relationship with him. We want you to be able to hold up your head and be proud of what he really stood for and fought for," said Henry.

"Yes," said Perry, "he was a champion who gave all that he had to assist George Washington achieve the dream Americans wanted. Even though things turned out badly for Arnold, it was for the best."

Thank you for giving me such a gift, boys. I can only say that I will write my book with an open mind, full of love for the Connecticut man who helped America truly become 'one nation under God'".

Henry hugged Miss Floon as she dabbed her eyes to catch tears of joy and relief that she had kept inside her heart for so many years.

***

They were knocking for what seemed like forever. All The Malt Shop gang were there, standing in the warm sunshine of late March outside the residence.

Finally, the door opened and someone pushed on the screen.

"Yes? Can I help you?" Mrs. Martin said.

Perry spoke first.

"Mrs. Martin, we are Sylvia's friends at the school. We have something we wanted to share with you. About Sylvia."

"Please come in; excuse the state of the house, I haven't been that organized this past year. My husband is in the hospital again, he never got over it you know."

"We understand that Sylvia's death was a dreadful shock and terrible loss to you both."

Now it was Charmaine's turn.

"We want you to know that she has never been far from our thoughts and prayers, Mrs. Martin. We miss her wonderful sense of humor…"

"…and her amazing musical talent," Rita broke in.

"The school orchestra never really could replace her," said Margot, who was also a cellist.

"What we mean to say is that you are not alone—I mean, in your grief and loss. We share it with you," said Charmaine.

Tears welled up in Mrs. Martin's eyes that would not stop.

"I…I never knew anyone felt what we felt, the loss of someone so dear," Mrs. Martin said between sobs.

Charmaine and Rita moved to sit close by her on the sofa.

Henry and Max and Perry knelt on the carpet in front.

Margot took her hand and gently laid it flat on her own knee.

From a small cloth pouch she drew forth a small object that caught the sun through the window just for a second in a flash of silver.

"We have reason to believe that this was lost by your daughter the night she died," said Perry. "Is it familiar at all?"

Mrs. Martin gasped, then closed her hand and brought it to her chest.

"We gave her this locket on her sixteenth birthday," she said. "Yes, of course I know it. How did you find it?"

Robert took his turn, to explain the search in the creek the day after at Lantern Bridge.

"We spotted it in the streambed and honestly did not know—until now," he said, taking her other hand in his.

"This is closure for us, too," said Margot, and all heads were nodding in agreement.

They had also all agreed not to mention the ghostly figure that had frightened and bewildered them that night on Lantern Bridge.

"So we return a small part of her to you, Mrs. Martin, with all our love and sympathy."

For a moment there was a deep peace in that room.

Without warning, the window in the dining room flew right open and a strong breeze blew the white chiffon curtains apart.

Without a word, they knew that Sylvia too was at peace at last.